A.J. had trusted Dan. She'd even let herself love him. How could he have betrayed her?

The things Dan had said in the newspaper interview—as well as the things he had done and the associations he'd had—were unforgivable. A.J. realized that she had only one choice.

Grimly determined, she started her Corvette and drove back to the speedway. She unlocked the office and set about the business of figuring up Dan's hours, wages, and withholdings. Quickly she wrote out the check and tucked it into an envelope.

Tires crunched on the gravel in the parking lot. It was Dan.

With a thundering heart, A.J. stood beside the door, waiting for him to alight. When Dan slammed the door of his Thunderbird, A.J. saw that he, too, had purchased a copy of the *News*. As pale as his features were, she knew that he had read the article. He would know exactly why she was so upset.

Closing her eyes in resolve, brushing away what tears lingered, she steeled herself to what had to be done.

A.J. wrenched the office door open.

Dan looked in her direction.

She rushed to him before he could say a word. Thrusting the envelope containing severance pay into his hand, A.J. announced with icy calm, "You're fired."

BRENDA BANCROFT is a pen name of inspirational romance author Susan Feldhake. At home in central Illinois with her husband, Steven, and four children, she is employed as a writing instructor for a college-accredited correspondence school. In her spare time she likes to hike, listen to country and western music, and fellowship with close friends.

Books by Brenda Bancroft

ROMANCE READER—TWO BOOKS IN ONE (under the pen name Susan Feldhake)

RR7—For Love Alone & Love's Sweet Promise

Indy Girl

Brenda Bancroft

Heartsong Presents

ISBN 1-55748-389-2

INDY GIRL

PRINTED IN U.S.A.

one

Amanda Jane Stacy snapped the closures of her leather racing gloves and secured the cuffs of her sleek jacket made of wind-resistant material. She tucked her shoulder-length brunette hair beneath the scuffed crash helmet and slipped unattractive goggles into place over her blue, long-lashed eyes.

Sighing, A.J. slid into the driver's seat of her late father's best race car. She seldom drove it because she was saving it for the day when she would fulfill the Stacy legacy and race over a Memorial Day weekend at the famous Brickyard in central Indiana, the Indianapolis 500.

A.J. sought a position of comfort behind the specially shaped wheel. She cocked her head, listening intently to the sounds of the racer's engine system. The noises reached her through a mesh guard which was located where a front windshield would be in an ordinary passenger car.

Taking a deep breath, A.J. eased the racer into gear and stepped lightly on the accelerator. The car catapulted smoothly toward the starting line painted across the track. The raceway stretched before A.J. Bleached white over the years by the blazing sun, the concrete oval threw out a silent challenge.

A tingle of excitement rippled through the racing-family heiress, pulsing all the way to her fingertips. The twenty-six-year-old driver knew her adrenaline had kicked in like a personal overdrive system. She was primed to spar with speed, her personal reflexes at peak performance.

A.J. drew another deep breath to calm herself, and she felt her pulse slow to a well-paced cadence. With a steady hand, she reached for the stopwatch beside her on the leather seat. She leaned forward, adjusting her restraint system, then glanced over her shoulder at the fuel cell, located in what would be a passenger car's back seat area.

The specially constructed fuel cell protected the race driver from risks associated with a rupturing gas tank. The fuel cell—petro contained within plastic, encased in steel, wrapped in mesh, and protected by styrofoam—had a mechanical system that activated a stop-leak device if the racer rolled over. This spared the driver the prospect of a fiery bath in gasoline.

A moment later, A.J. halted the metallic blue racer precisely at the painted line. Her pulse continued to solidly thud, as if it were ticking down the seconds. Imaginary green flags sliced the gentle breeze, signalling "Go!"

With a deft movement, A.J. punched the mechanism of the stopwatch, hit the gas, and shot ahead. She was the lone driver on the wide, sun-baked slab her father, veteran race driver Rick Stacy, had constructed so many years earlier. Before his tragic death, he had made Stacy Speedway one of the most respected stock car raceways in the nation.

At one time, A.J., Rick Stacy's only surviving child, had known exactly how many cubic yards of cement had gone into the racetrack's construction. She had even known how many tons of steel reinforcing wire had been required to guard the track against nature's freeze and thaw cycles.

But passing years had a way of erasing statistics from the mind, just as the relentless advance of time had a way of dimming personal memories. While A.J. could no longer remember the exact amount of material used in creating the speedway, however, one thought she could not put from mind—would not put from her mind. She dreamed that within twenty-four months a Stacy racer would be in the starting lineup at the Indy 500.

A.J. renewed this vow each time she visited the graves of her father and brother, well-respected, dedicated drivers who had both died speeding toward culmination of that family dream.

As the only surviving member of the illustrious racing Stacys, it was up to Amanda Jane to accomplish the feat.

Snapping her mind shut, as if she, too, had a device to prevent potentially dangerous leaks, A.J. halted thoughts of the past and concentrated on the upcoming turn. It was the first she would face as she sped around the oval track.

She glanced up at the speedometer. A row of gauges and dummy lights spanned the area where a visor would have been located in the average family auto. This setup made it easier for a driver soaring around the track to check internal conditions without looking away from the raceway.

Into the second lap, A.J. hadn't begun to wring from the engine what she knew was possible. But the track wasn't as long as the Indy 500. Nor was the racer insured for its full worth, due to her accountant's insistence she cut overhead where she could. So sanity mingled with sentimentality, and A.J. refrained from giving her car free rein.

But the day was coming, she knew, when she'd seek from the sleek racer all that it had to give, and she'd ask no less of herself. In the meantime, she made a mental note to up the coverage on the car now that she'd begun implementing her step-by-step plan that would surely win her a slot in the starting lineup at the Indy two years away.

By the third lap, the car was crooning a sweet song. A.J.'s ears told her that all systems were working at their peak. The racer shot effortlessly around the track.

A.J. smiled to herself as she considered how the way in which you were raised dictated what you knew and listened for. Her right-hand office administrator, Beth Carter, had taken eleven years of piano lessons as a child and played the organ for church services. Her sense of hearing was so well developed that when a radio announcer identified an upcoming song, Beth would start humming it in the right key before the melody began playing over the speakers.

Absorbed with her thoughts, A.J. didn't notice the onlooker at the fence, his booted foot resting on a brace post that secured the stout enclosure surrounding the track. Only as she wrapped up her fourth lap did she spot him. She processed the information gleaned from that brief glimpse as she did the signals she was receiving from the dummy lights and gauges.

The man was tall—taller than she. He was lean, but muscular. His hair was brown, but the tips were light, sun-streaked. His skin was burned bronze, as if he worked outside or had recently returned from a fun-in-the-sun vacation. Not only that, but he was older, A.J. realized. Old enough to be interesting.

Into her fifth lap, A.J. prepared to take another look and gave a sharp glance to the side, straining for a better impression of her onlooker. She wasn't sure if their gazes locked for an instant, but she felt her heart lurch before she jerked her eyes back to the track and roared on down the straightaway. She held to the inside, suddenly feeling like a high school girl showing off for a potential boyfriend.

A.J. felt oddly unnerved, the spell of the speedway broken. She wasn't sure why. After all, it wasn't as if she were unaccustomed to being watched. When she'd raced at tracks across the United States and Canada, bleachers were crammed with hundreds, even thousands, of cheering onlookers.

And even around Stacy Speedway, it wasn't uncommon to have a gaggle of lank and gawky teenage boys jostling for a better viewing position at

the fence as they admiringly watched the lady
driver put her stock cars through their paces. A.J.
knew that had the usual boys been visitors at the
speedway that morning, they would have considered it a major treat to see her behind the wheel of
legendary Rick Stacy's racer. And she would have
allowed them to inspect the car in detail when
she'd concluded her run.

They were such good kids, she thought, recalling
them with fondness. Sometimes the boys seemed
like younger brothers. She enjoyed their teasing,
reciprocating with plenty of her own. But after
they'd all gone home to their families and Beth
had departed for the day, A.J. remained alone in
the speedway office. During those quiet evenings,
she was often struck by the notion that there really
should be more to life than what she knew.

Several of the boys had given her their high
school class pictures, while blushingly asking A.J.
for her autographed publicity shot in full racing
regalia. Sometimes late at night while she sat in
the office catching up on speedway business,
she'd stop to give her weary eyes a rest and her
gaze would fall on those class photos. Without fail
she'd be gripped by the fact that there was no one
to whom she could pass on the Stacy legend and
lore. Would her father's legacy end with her?

Thankfully, those bleak moments were few and
far between. Generally A.J. countered such mel-
ancholy by throwing herself more wholeheartedly
into the work required to maintain the family
business that had become her sole enterprise. As a

result, Stacy Speedway flourished as it had back in the days when Rick Stacy was at the helm, and of this fact, A.J. was understandably proud.

But there was a trade-off—as it seemed there always was. Time sped by faster each year, and with her thirtieth birthday just around the next curve in the road of life, she was reminded that opportunities were escaping. Some things would be forever denied her. Some choices offered no second chance.

As a younger woman, before her brother Kip's death, A.J. had believed that someday she'd meet a special man, fall in love, wed, and start a family of little racing enthusiasts.

Now she wasn't so sure.

There were those—especially A.J.'s good friend Jill Alexander and Beth—who accused A.J. of being married to her work. They saw A.J.'s stock cars as her surrogate children. Blithely A.J. admitted that they were right. She was committed to racing the way others were dedicated to maintaining varied relationships.

But what she couldn't admit to anyone, sometimes not even to herself, was that her life had an almost unbearable void. A.J. realized that to onlookers it seemed her life was filled with excitement, activity, fame, and fortune. But as much as A.J. Stacy knew she had, there were moments when she felt as if she possessed nothing of value.

Before the deaths of her father and brother, A.J. had desired for herself the exact future she now claimed. But what had once been a young girl's passionate dream had become a mature woman's inherited profession with many nightmarish aspects. She was no longer certain that it was what she actually wanted.

For A.J. Stacy, racing was no longer an exciting and enjoyable occupation. It had become an exhausting obsession. Regardless of her inner turmoil, however, people depended on her. For their sakes, she was obligated to live out the reality bequeathed to her.

Beneath her goggles, A.J.'s eyes suddenly stung and grew misty. She tried to tell herself that it was from the force of the wind. But of course that was absurd. She was crying.

The fail-safe device she'd tried to activate to prevent a trickle of memories had failed. Helplessly she considered what other women possessed. Even as the Stacy dream glowed bright, A.J. found herself wanting what average women took for granted in simple, everyday family life. Even if they were undergoing financial difficulties, they were rich in a way money couldn't buy. They had each other. A.J. Stacy had no one.

Kip. Her dad. Her parents' marriage. The Stacy family's lifestyle had cost them everything. It had been too high a price to pay.

Most of the time, A.J. coped with her loneliness by staying very busy, but at times she was bitter, especially when she considered the circumstances surrounding Kip's accident. Rage and a desire for revenge smoldered when she thought of the man responsible for Kip's death, a one-time friend turned enemy. He'd been among the finalists that year, but only because he'd cut her brother off on the track, jockeying for a better position. He had forced Kip to hit the brakes. Kip's car had skidded across the track until it was broadsided by another racer. The car had flipped into the wall, and Kip had died on impact.

Rick Stacy had forgiven the driver. A.J. could not. Even now, a half a dozen years later, she still missed her older brother. She firmly believed that Kip's one-time best friend was a greedy traitor, willing to pay any price to win.

Drawn together in their grief, A.J. and her father had become inseparable. A.J.'s mother had reacted in a different way. She had declared that had it not been for the Stacy Legacy—what she scathingly termed an obsession—Kip might still be with them. Unable to bear the probability of becoming yet another race car driver's widow, Rick Stacy's wife had distanced herself. Eventually she had become a divorcee.

Three years later, Rick Stacy had died in an accident.

A.J.'s mother, Liz, remained estranged, although A.J. was aware that the differences were as much her fault as her mother's. The day-in-day-out ache of hurt and loss were more than mere words could begin to convey. A.J. missed family ties.

Lap seven was beginning as A.J. reached up to swipe at the moisture clinging to the bottom of her goggles. Mentally she ordered herself to cut it out, for racing around a concrete slab at 120 miles per hour was neither the time nor place for a good cry, even if she needed one. And need one she did, for lately, nothing had seemed to go right.

It was almost as if she were jinxed. No sooner had she set in motion the carefully delineated plan to take her from Stacy Speedway to the Brickyard in Indianapolis, than things had begun to go awry. It was as if there were a power greater than she who was flatly and firmly saying no.

When a frustrated A.J. had cried on Beth's shoulder, the older woman had taken it as an opportunity to sermonize. She'd told the lonely woman that perhaps her plans were going wrong because she wasn't pursuing the purpose God had for her life.

A.J. had chewed her lip to contain sharp words when a soothing-voiced Beth had pointed out that if A.J. were meant to race in the Indy, she'd get there effortlessly. And if A.J. were not meant to participate in the five-hundred-mile race, then she'd fail to reach her goal no matter how hard she tried.

"So why not leave it up to the Lord and do as He would choose, hon?" Beth had kindly suggested. "Trust in Him to show you the way."

A.J. was the tough lady boss of Stacy Speedway, and the wavering indecisiveness that Beth suggested almost made her laugh out loud. It hadn't been easy as a pretty woman to make it in a man's world. Stacy Speedway employees knew to do her bidding, or explain exactly why not. She'd been in control for the past two years, making all the decisions, facing all the risks, accepting good fortune the same way she endured bad luck.

A.J. Stacy was so accustomed to being in charge that she could not imagine relying on anyone else. Not even God.

two

A.J. noticed that the onlooker was still present a moment before she streaked across the finish line and depressed the button on the stopwatch.

She wondered what he wanted. He was old enough that she suspected he was there on some sort of business, not killing time like her friends from area high schools did.

A.J.'s heart skipped a beat when she considered that perhaps the man was there to fill out a job application. But her hopes sank as quickly as they had soared when she realized that wasn't possible. It had only been a week since she'd given Beth ad copy and instructed her to place it with the *Racers' Edge* magazine, a trade journal. The ad wouldn't appear for a few more days.

That had been A.J.'s first step in replacing her mechanic and in looking for a manager to take over some of her duties behind the desk. She hoped she would be able to find someone who could free her up to spend more time behind the wheel competing in her various race cars.

A.J. drove another lap around the track, letting the racer's own momentum propel it. Then she rolled around into another lap, going slower and slower. Finally she cruised to a stop in the pit area.

As she swiveled on the seat to unbuckle her restraint system, she tossed a glance toward where the man had been standing. He was proceeding in her direction.

Slowly she unwound from the sleek, low-slung car. Easing the kinks from her body, A.J. stood to her full height and regarded the man through goggle-protected eyes.

"Hi!" he called out, waving.

A.J. lifted a hand in lieu of speaking.

He strode toward her.

"Nice day for a run," he said as an opening gambit.

As he drew close to her, A.J. removed the goggles. She was glad that, perhaps because she'd felt unusually bleak and had hoped it would lift her spirits, she'd given herself the full makeup treatment that morning: foundation, powder, blush, eyebrow pencil, shadow, liner, mascara. She'd even sprayed on some ridiculously expensive perfume, a birthday gift from her mother.

Although her features remained expressionless, inwardly A.J. chuckled when she detected the startled look wash over the handsome man's face. She felt like a magician who'd just segued into his best trick as with a flourish she removed the helmet and shook free her thick, dark hair. The waves swirled in the faint breeze and cascaded at shoulder level.

The man was as surprised as A.J. had known he would be.

She smiled. "Can I help you?" she asked.

Silence spun a moment longer as the man continued to stare.

"Uh, yeah. I'm looking for A.J. Stacy, ma'am. Can you tell me where I can find him?"

She extended her hand. "You're talking to her. I'm A.J. What can I do for you?"

"I'm relocating to this area, so I'm looking for a job in the field I know. An acquaintance told me about Stacy Speedway. The name's Dan Barenfanger."

"Nice to meet you, Dan. Just call me A.J. Everyone else does," she murmured. Taking advantage of the fact that they were finally facing each other, she gave the man a quick, scrutinizing look.

A jumble of perceptions passed through her mind and then began to sort themselves into what amounted to a first impression. Admittedly, the man presented a good image.

"We've got ads slated seeking both a mechanic and a general manager. Which position were you interested in, Dan?"

He gave her a shrug and lopsided smile. "Either one or both."

A.J. wanted to say, "Surely you jest," but she bit the words back. Instead, she frowned reflectively. "Both, hmmm. Really? That's a pretty tough order. Do you think you can handle it?"

"I wouldn't have suggested it if I didn't believe myself capable. Before I watched you make laps, I looked around a bit. I think I can do the job. Either one. Or both. That is, unless the racer you were in is atypical. I noticed it was in great shape. It wouldn't take a lot of maintenance—just preventative work—to keep it ready for peak performance. Unless the other racers in your fleet are clunkers—"

"Afraid not," A.J. broke in, laughing. "And there isn't a lot of mechanical work, but I do need someone. I can't do it all. My former mechanic left to sign on with a team bound for the Indy 500."

She managed to keep her voice neutral, not giving in to the grating emotion she felt that the man had left her employ to go over to work for *him*. The man who'd caused Kip's crash.

"Since then I've been serving as my own grease monkey as well as race track manager. Now I'm at the point where I'd really like to have a manicure last for longer than thirty minutes," she admitted and gave a girlish laugh.

"See?" he said. "Apparently one person can do it."

"But I've known this business since I was this high," A.J. said, gesturing down around her knees.

"In some ways, so've I," Dan admitted. "I've been associated with racing families in the past. I used to drive, too, but I gave that up and settled for working in peripheral areas."

"I could always try to help out if you got into a bind," A.J. murmured as she began to give the situation serious consideration.

There were appealing aspects to hiring one individual to fill both jobs. There would be less paperwork. Her accountant would shriek with ecstacy over the reduced overhead. Instead of the speedway picking up the benefits for two employees, it would be adding only one name to the payroll.

"You've done work with stock cars?" A.J. asked. "That's our main thrust around here, our bread and butter business. But we've an interest in grooming for the big races. Specifically, the Indy. That's why I feel a bit upset that my mechanic left me for another team instead of sticking around for a Stacy to return to the Brickyard. Any experience in stocks?"

"It's where I cut my teeth," Dan admitted. "Then I went on to help a guy who was heading for the big time—the Indy. He didn't make it, but another guy I was close to did, and I was in his pit crew at Indy. That was a long time ago. But some things don't change. I handled the work and tension then, and I know I can take care of it when you're ready to hit the bricks."

"Great," A.J. said. "Then there should be no problems. I'm a good boss and a fair one."

"I haven't had any complaints about my personality or my professional performance," Dan quietly replied. "So I don't anticipate any problems. And A.J., if the Indy 500 is where your future lies, then I'd see it as my duty to help you get there. Safely."

"I like that attitude, Dan. If you've been around racetracks, then you know that the days can be long, the work demanding, and the attention to detail a relentless requirement. We won't be able to guarantee you banker's hours."

"I wouldn't be applying for work at Stacy Speedway if I wasn't prepared to handle that, too."

A.J. asked careful questions, and with each

answer, she found herself liking Dan better. She was as impressed with his personality as she was by his professional qualifications. Although he spoke of them in a modest manner, A.J. had detected that Dan's abilities were very solid.

"We allow no smoking at Stacy Speedway except in a designated room off the office building," she pointed out.

"No problem there," Dan said. "I'm a non-smoker."

"Me, too," Stacy said. "And if you ever show up with alcohol on your breath or hide a bottle in with the containers of brake fluid or behind an oil drum, then you're history. Got that?" Her warning was stern, although from outward appearances she judged it was probably unnecessary.

He nodded. "I'm not a drinker, either."

"Okay. One more question," A.J. added. She knew the answer to this question would help her gauge the moral tone Dan would bring to the work environment. Any new employee could reinforce the bond a team needed, or cause it to erode—a dangerous situation when lives were at stake. She wanted to make sure that Dan saw her as a driver, not simply as an attractive woman. Even if he recognized her as a pretty face, A.J. wanted to know that he was professional enough not to try to mix romance and racing.

A.J. swallowed hard, for this question was one she dreaded. In the past she'd had absolutely marvelous interviews fall apart at this point, and she hoped that Dan Barenfanger's would not be one of them.

Her trick question was one she never asked unless she was almost positive she was going to offer the applicant a job. It was potentially too humiliating. An otherwise qualified professional would sometimes respond to it with ribald humor, especially if there happened to be other men around. He might be more interested in impressing them with macho remarks than in impressing her with a professional attitude.

"How are you at body work?"

To A.J.'s relief, Dan didn't wink or leer at her or offer to give her a demonstration as a few potential mechanics had in the past. He seemed unaware of the question's potential for being given a double meaning.

"I'm not the world's best," he admitted, "but neither am I the world's worst. I'd assume with your Indy-bound racer that it's a matter of replacing fiberglass parts. With the assembly-line stocks, what couldn't be easily replaced I could fabricate with body repair materials. I'm pretty handy with an air brush to touch up paint jobs. And I'm good at straightening frames, even if they're crooked as a dog's hind leg. It's time-consuming work, but you already know that.

"Again, A.J., I really don't foresee problems. It looked to me like you're a good driver. I don't anticipate you cracking up on the track. Or hitting a wall."

A.J.'s thoughts flicked to the past. She gave a shrug that she hoped would help dislodge the sudden dry lump in her throat when she thought of

Kip's accident. So many considered it to have been avoidable, while others viewed it as an unfortunate instance of human error: nothing more, nothing less. And there was Rick Stacy's crash, equally unexpected.

"No one ever anticipates hitting the wall, Dan. No one."

"Maybe that's why I gave up racing myself a couple years ago," he said. "I started to anticipate it. Or at least consider it a possibility in a way I never had before. I began to question the wisdom of streaking down the straightaway. Before long, I quit driving. But the tracks are in my blood, A.J., the same way that they are in yours. Now I serve the purpose I feel I was created for, simply in a race-related capacity."

A.J. looked at Dan, and somehow she knew his wasn't a case of cowardice or losing nerve. There was some other motivation that had driven Dan Barenfanger to give up driving, but it wasn't up to her to pry. She knew what it was like to be in the public eye, and she savored what privacy could be had. It was a right she extended to others.

"You're hired if you want the job, Dan. When can you begin?"

"When would you like me to start?"

A.J. gave a rueful laugh. "Last week would've been marvelous, Dan. But tomorrow will do. Stop by the office in the morning and fill out all the paperwork for Beth. I'll show you around first thing, and you'll officially become a part of the Stacy Speedway team. I think you'll like the others. We've a small staff here, but we're like family.

"I might warn you about Beth Carter. She likes to mother-hen us all. Sometimes I think if that woman has any faults it's in caring too much. So don't get your back up and feel offended if she invites you to attend church services. Beth's a dear and she truly means well. She wants for everyone what she has for herself, I guess. So don't make any quick judgments and decide you don't like Beth. She's probably the most wonderful woman I know."

Dan Barenfanger laughed. "She sounds like my kind of person." Then he changed the subject. "Uh, before I go, aren't we even going to discuss wages?"

Uncharacteristically, A.J. shrugged it off. "Tell Beth what you want in terms of hourly compensation. She'll fill you in on the benefits we can offer."

"Good enough," Dan agreed, although from the look he gave her, A.J. knew he seemed to find it a bit unusual that an employer was so confident and trusting.

"See you tomorrow, Dan. And welcome to the Indy Girl's team!"

"Glad to be a part of it," he called after her as A.J. strode toward her racer to put it away. Then Dan turned and headed toward the gate to let himself into the parking area.

Somehow A.J. knew that Dan Barenfanger wouldn't inflate his value to her. There was some-

thing about him that appealed to her. Something
that reassured her sense of women's intuition. He
was a man to trust. She could have faith in him.

And he'd come to the Stacy Speedway just in
time, as if he were custom-made to fill the slot.
Added to that, A.J. sensed that Dan Barenfanger
and Beth Carter would get along A-Okay.

No doubt Beth, bless her heart, was going to
consider the tall, handsome man to be a gift from
God. Of that, A.J. was positive because even she,
non-church-going Amanda Jane Stacy, had already
labeled Dan just that.

three

After Dan's departure, A.J. went about her business, all the while considering what it would cost to employ a man of Dan's caliber. She recalled her latest meeting with her perennially gloomy accountant. With a wry sigh she anticipated screams in the near future when he poured over Stacy Speedway books and discovered what it was going to cost to capitalize her sufficiently for a shot at the Indy 500. But the news she'd made a two-in-one deal should appeal to him. Somehow she'd find other ways to cut overhead so that money could be diverted to fund her dream.

With sudden purpose, A.J. slammed the door to the racer and jogged toward the office where Beth was straightening up her desk preparatory to leaving for the day.

"Something wrong?" the older woman inquired when A.J. bolted into the room. A.J. dropped into her chair, aglow with a burst of efficiency and aiming to increase production and trim any remaining flab from her business routine.

"No!" she replied, grinning, out of breath. "Suddenly everything seems very, very right, as a matter of fact. A mechanic, with experience servicing race cars, just walked in off the street and applied for a job. Not only that, but he's also going to fill in as our general manager to free me up to shoot for the Indy."

Beth whistled low. "Wow! He must be quite a fellow."

A.J. rocked back in the huge chair. "I was very impressed."

Beth's eyebrows shot up. "That impresses me."

A.J. swiveled to face her and toyed with a gold pen. "How so?"

Beth gave a wry chuckle. "Because you, my dear, are not exactly easily impressed."

A.J. cocked her head. "That's true. But I have a good feeling about Dan. I think that we're going to get this speedway running as never before."

"How about your personal life? Going to get that running smoothly, too?"

"That, my dear Mrs. Carter, is an impertinent question. Anyway, how should I know about my personal life? I don't have a crystal ball. And I'm not a believer in horoscopes."

"Thank God for that," Beth replied. "I just thought you might know if there was the same chemistry between you two on a personal level that you seem to have in the professional realm. I thought maybe he would constitute someone we on the staff could consider 'eligible.' There aren't that many unattached men in your age bracket. At least not the kind a nice girl would want."

"You're an incorrigible matchmaker. There's a meeting of the minds, Beth, but that's all. I know nothing about Dan on a personal level. For that matter he's probably as attached as everyone else. He no doubt has a devoted wife and a passel of adoring children."

"You mean you didn't even ask?"

" 'Fraid not, Bethie. That's none of my concern.

What I'm interested in is employing a top-notch mechanic and a conscientious manager. And that's what I know I'm going to get."

"But wouldn't it be wonderful if you'd get a boy-friend thrown in for free?"

"Would it?" A.J. asked quietly and gave Beth a long look. "I, for one, don't know about that." She lifted her face and her chin grew rigid. "I happen to like my life just the way it is," she defended stoutly.

"I give up!" Beth sighed. "You're exasperating. Every bit your father's daughter." Chuckling, she reached for her jacket. "So what's this miracle worker going to cost us?"

"We haven't discussed wages."

"You weren't kidding when you said you didn't get at all personal with him, A.J.! I can't believe you."

"I told Dan—his last name is Barenfanger—to inform you what he wanted in terms of compensation, and that's what we'd pay."

"Barenfanger?" Beth squinted at A.J. "Do we know him? That name sort of rings a bell."

A.J. gave a disinterested shrug. "It meant nothing to me."

Beth tweaked A.J.'s cheek. "At the risk of sounding flip, lovey, you haven't been keeping records in racing for as long as I have or fielding as many telephone calls. Maybe I've just got my wires crossed and I'm confusing his name with something similar."

"Well, come the morrow you can find out whatever personal stats you'd like to know about Dan.

When he completes tax deduction paperwork, you'll
know his marital status and how many dependents he
has."

"Or doesn't have," Beth added, a hopeful note in
her tone.

"Don't scare him off, Bethie. I want a mechanic
and a manager. Please don't give him the impression
that I'm in the market to find someone to marry! I
promise you: I'm not going to agree to pay him that
well," A.J. added with a laugh.

"You know, in the wrong hands, A.J., such a carte
blanche financial arrangement could be quite
dangerous."

"I know. But somehow, I also know that Dan's not
going to be like that. I can tell that he'll deliver a
full measure for wages given. I'm not concerned."

"Your accountant might be. You know how he's
been lately. Nagging—I mean trying very hard to
help us find ways to safeguard our profit line."

A.J. shot the wall clock an impassioned glance,
mentally calculated for crossing two time zones, and
gave a thin cry.

"Quick, Beth! Dial the advertising department
head at the *Racers' Edge* in California. We can
cancel the ad we had slated. The deadline for display ad copy isn't until tomorrow. Maybe they can
send back our uncancelled check, refund the
money, or—"

"They won't—"

"What!" A.J. tossed down her pen in disappointment. The half-page display ad had cost her more
than she generally would have considered laying

out, but she had been desperate. That money represented wasted funds that the accountant could happily cry over for months.

"Do they have a policy of no refunds?" she asked Beth.

Beth lowered her gaze. She toyed with the clasp on her purse.

"What I started to say, A.J., is that they won't have to refund the ad money—"

"But Beth, it's superfluous to let them run the ad now. I'm positive Dan's going to work out," A.J. interrupted a second time. "There's no sense wasting our time, nor the efforts and expenses of optimistic applicants, either. Maybe if I talk to the department head personally, they'll at least agree to refund half the fee—"

"A.J., hear me out. I have a confession to make."

Silence spiraled between them.

"Beth, what are you talking about?" A.J. asked, studying the older woman who'd been like a mother and grandmother and favorite aunt rolled into one.

"I never sent off the advertising copy."

"What!" A.J. gasped. "Beth, that's not like you! You absolutely never forget something so important."

"It wasn't an oversight. It was intentional."

A shocked A.J. jumped to her feet and then dropped back into her battered office chair. She was momentarily speechless.

"I told you that I was going to pray about it," Beth admitted in a soft voice. "And I asked my prayer partners to bring it to the Lord in their petitions, too."

"Beth, I can't believe you," A.J. exclaimed, confused.

She knew that she should be angry over Beth's ignoring office procedure and the work order of a business day, but instead, she felt like laughing. What could have been a financial disaster had turned out like a dream come true. It evaporated her potential for fury.

"We were trusting that God would provide," Beth said. "And He did."

"You squeaked through this time, Beth," A.J. said. "But what if your Lord hadn't?"

Beth shrugged. "Then I suppose that I could have faxed the advertising copy to the magazine and asked them to bill us for payment."

A.J. gave a rueful laugh. "You always have an answer, don't you?"

"Yes, I do have the Answer," Beth said. "With God I know that all things are possible. Miracles are His stock in trade."

"Sometimes I think you're impossible," A.J. growled, but she recognized that Beth knew she wasn't as dismayed as she tried to appear.

"Is there anything you'd like me to do before I leave?" Beth asked.

"Not that I can think of," A.J. replied, yawning. "I'll be leaving before long myself."

"Don't forget to turn on the answering machine."

A.J. pressed a button. "It's on now. I can intercept the machine while I work. See you tomorrow, Beth. Have a nice evening."

"I'm sure I will. You too."

"I'll try," A.J. replied in a bright tone, even as she felt a sensation of weariness when she realized that the long hours ahead would be a duplicate of many others. Indistinguishable. Boring. Lonely.

After Beth's departure, A.J. sighed and bent over some paperwork, intent on clearing it from the desk as quickly as she could. Then she would leave for the apartment that was merely a place to eat and sleep. It had never felt like home. Idly she hoped that there would be something good on television to help pass the long evening hours alone.

Her social life was a vast wasteland. A love life was nonexistent.

She'd lost touch with most of her high school friends. They'd gone off to college, studied for interesting careers, and moved away. Or else they'd married local boys and settled down. But they were so busy with in-laws, raising small children, and entertaining new friends their husbands worked with that A.J. felt they had no time for her. Some of her old friends seemed to live in such neatly paired sets that A.J. felt like an odd man out whenever she was in her married friends' company.

There were a few women she knew, single, like herself, but they were different, too. Most of them, having suffered one failed relationship, were on the prowl to try again, hoping for better success the second time around. A.J. found that she had little in common with them, and she was unsettled by the desperation she detected in them. Somehow she felt even more bleak in their company.

Jerking her musings from that avenue, A.J. tried to

force her thoughts down more productive routes. She frowned as she struggled to focus harder on what she was doing.

No sooner had she begun to succeed than the telephone shrilled, breaking her concentration. She was tempted to let the machine get it, figuring that it was someone calling to inquire about race schedules or ticket information. They often got calls from people who phoned the office instead of the number especially programmed to dispense such data. Grudgingly, A.J. reached for the phone.

"Hello, Indy Girl! This is Jill," she heard when she answered.

"Hi! What're you up to?" A.J. asked, surprised and delighted. "Long time no see."

"That's what I'm calling about," Jill admitted. "We're both so busy in our own little worlds that it seems our orbits don't cross as frequently as I wish they did."

"I know what you mean. So how's everything?"

"I got a promotion at work," Jill said.

"Great!" A.J. said. "That's one of the drawbacks of being your own boss. Once you're there, you've gone about as far as you can go."

"You're not giving up on the Indy, are you?"

"Oh, heavens, no. You know what I mean, though."

"There are some perks in addition to the pay raise. Now that I have a promotion, I'm covering more interesting news events. I'm not relegated to the boring beat of city council meetings and the like. That means that my evenings are free more often than they used to be."

"That's music to my ears, Jill. I've really missed you. One of these evenings we simply must get away, get together, and have supper at some nice place. I mean that."

"Same here. I don't suppose, busy as you are with the speedway, that you'd be able to bop out for a quick dinner tonight?"

"Well, as a matter of fact, I'm going to be locking up in a little while, and the only prospect I have at home is television and a dinner to match. A meal out has definite appeal."

"Then we're on?"

"Green flags all the way," A.J. agreed.

"Great! Tell me when and where, and I'll be there."

"Is Granny's Kitchen all right? The food's super, and the atmosphere is subdued enough so that we can talk. My treat," A.J. stipulated.

"But I'm the one who called in hopes of us getting together," Jill protested.

"You can buy next time."

"Okay," Jill agreed, "because there is going to be a next time. We're going to see each other as often as we can while we've got the chance."

"Count on it."

"See you in a jiff, A.J. And be prepared to make a night of it. We've got a lot of catching up to do. Things have really been happening in my life. In fact, I have a favor to ask."

"Anything. Now you've got me curious."

"I hope you'll agree."

"You have to know by now that whatever you

want, if it's in my power to accomplish it, 'tis good as done."

"Super. I think you'll be surprised when you hear the details."

"I'll meet you at Granny's in about an hour, my dear, and you can tell me all about it."

"See you then!"

four

A.J. swung her white Corvette into the parking lot of Granny's Kitchen a moment after Jill parked.

Quickly the two women secured their vehicles and exchanged hugs in the parking lot made bright with overhead security lights.

A.J. held Jill at arm's length, then shook her head in admiring amazement. "You've always been a pretty girl, but now you're looking even better."

"I feel even better, too," Jill said, falling into step with A.J. They walked briskly toward the entrance of the quaint, three-story Victorian home that had been renovated into Granny's Kitchen.

A.J. held the door open for both of them. "There's something different about you. I can't quite put my finger on it."

"My hairdo?" Jill fluffed her tresses.

"No, I've seen you since you went to a shorter style."

A.J. made several more guesses, while Jill looked more amused by the moment. The hostess was approaching when a teasing smile lit up the journalist's features.

"Give up?"

"I'm crying 'Uncle,' " A.J. agreed with a nod

and held up two fingers to the hostess who beckoned them to follow her.

"My dear, it's probably what is called 'the look of love,' " Jill said in a mysterious tone.

"What!"

Jill extended her left hand. A lovely diamond gleamed from her ring finger.

A startled gasp escaped from A.J.'s lips. "You're engaged!" she cried.

"Uh-huh. And I've never been happier."

Although it was irrational, A.J. felt a stab of some odd emotion—envy?—even though she truly wanted nothing but the best for her girlhood friend.

A.J. gave Jill an impulsive hug before they were seated. "Who is the lucky guy? Anyone I know?"

"I don't think so. Rod McKitterick. He's a lawyer with a very prestigious firm in Chicago. So it looks like my days at the *Daily News* are numbered."

"Oh, Jill. I'm going to miss you!"

"That's what I hinted at over the telephone. We'll have to see more of each other while we've got the chance."

"Maybe we'll be like some people and see more of each other when we're parted by great distances than we've managed to while living in the same city."

"It could happen," Jill agreed as she opened her menu.

A.J. brushed her hair over her shoulders. She knew that there was almost a protocol that the occasion called for.

Quickly she scanned the list and made her choice, laying the menu aside to signal the waitress that she was ready to order.

"Where'd you meet Mr. Right?" she asked when Jill followed suit. "I haven't had much luck discovering a guy meant for me."

"Well, let me tell you, kiddo, Ann Landers is right when she says to skip the singles' bar scene, bypass the computer dating, and go where the nice men can be found: social charitable clubs, church organizations, and the like."

"No kidding? Where'd you meet Rod? Jaycees? Business and Professional Women?"

"At a church ice cream social."

"You? Jill, you're putting me on, aren't you? I mean—you—my liberated, liberal, free-thinking, independent, irreligious chum since our days in diapers?"

Jill laughed, but flushed. "I most certainly did meet him at a church social sponsored by a youth group. My landlady, you see, had agreed to sell some tickets. So to be a good scout I bought one from her, not planning on using it. The day of the social her car was in the shop. She was preparing to take a cab. I had nothing better to do, so offering to drive her seemed the right thing to do."

"Of course. But—"

"I've always had a weakness for ice cream—"

"So you weren't going to let that ticket go to waste," A.J. laughed.

"Correct. I marched in, redeemed my ticket,

and Mr. Right walked right into my life. My landlady's best friend, Hattie Davenport, just happened to have a weekend houseguest. Her nephew—"

"Rod McKitterick," A.J. finished for her.

"We met, we hit it off, we began to see each other, and—"

"The rest is history," A.J. said and there was a soft wistfulness to her tone.

Wordlessly Jill nodded.

"Ready to order?" The chipper waitress approached and the two career women turned their attention to that matter.

"So what's new with you?" Jill asked when they'd placed their orders and were left in privacy again.

"Same old same old," A.J. dismissed.

"How's business?"

"I can't complain."

"You're still going in circles, huh?" Jill cracked a joke.

"The day I stop they'll probably be carrying me out feet first, my dear."

Jill frowned. "Hmmm."

A.J., too, frowned. "What's with you, Jill? Something I said just provoked a reaction in you."

"Nothing, really," she murmured. "I just thought that maybe you were ripe for a career change."

"Now whatever on earth would give you that idea?" A.J. replied.

"Nothing. It was just an idle remark."

"Liar," A.J. said. "It was not. I know you better than that, Jill Alexander. You dropped that remark in front of me like the ace reporter you are—to see if I'd reach down and pick it up."

"And you did. So give me the scoop. Off the record if it has to be. But I won't let my closest girlfriend scoop to someone else."

A.J. rubbed her arms. "You're making me feel strange, Jill. As if my telephone is bugged or you've been reading my mail. You—you shouldn't be making oblique references to what I would imagine you'd know nothing about."

Jill gave a wee smile. "Now you're being oblique, A.J."

"Okay," A.J. sighed. "Tell me what you know, and I'll tell you what the situation is. Off the record," she stipulated, while hoping that what Jill would have to say would be rooted solely in fantasy. A.J. had some news of interest to a paper, but she had kept it from Beth, her accountant, everyone but the speedway's lawyer.

"Well, I heard that there was a chance you were going to sell Stacy Speedway."

"Wrong. That's an unfounded rumor."

"Was an offer made?"

"To my knowledge—no."

"To your knowledge? You don't know for certain?"

"This is all off the record, Jill," A.J. stipulated. "Remember?"

The reporter nodded.

"My attorney contacted me several weeks ago. He told me that someone had expressed interested in buying out Stacy Speedway. I told him that I absolutely, positively, was not in the market to sell. So, quite frankly, Jill, I don't know if they made the law firm an offer to suggest to me or not."

Jill nodded. "Very interesting. I wouldn't have known about it, hon, except the sportswriter for the *Daily News* knows that you and I have been longtime friends. He'd been tipped about a possible sale. He checked with me to see if I knew anything. And of course I didn't."

"So you saw to it that we got together for dinner so you could pump me?" A.J. helplessly flared.

"What kind of remark is that?" Jill snapped back, but immediately apologized for making it.

"I'm sorry, too," A.J. sighed. "Knowing that someone is interested in buying the speedway has made me think about it in a way I'd never considered before. I've started to get foolish and wonder if there could be a life after the race track."

"Of course there would be."

"But would I want it? I've been curious about the possibilities. I think maybe I should sell, then I consider the legacy Dad left me, and I know that I can't. Not yet, anyway."

"Oh, A.J. Do you want to be the Indy Girl for your father? Or for yourself?"

"For both. I think."

"Then you don't really know for sure?"

A.J. shook her head.

"So tell me, Jill," A.J. murmured a moment later, taking a sip of water to help her get rid of the catch she was afraid might appear in her voice. "Does your source in the sports room have information on who wants to buy Stacy Speedway?"

"Don't tell me that you don't know?"

"I wouldn't let our lawyer even discuss it to that extent," A.J. admitted. "But deep down, I think I know."

"We both know," Jill said. "It's Duke Carrington who wants to buy you out."

"I'd die before I'd let that happen," A.J. said, her tone low and hoarse with fury. "The audacity of that man! You know I hold him solely responsible for Kip's death. If Duke hadn't cut Kip off in that race! He shaved a few precious seconds off his race time, even though it meant the eternal end of the line for my brother."

Angry tears caused A.J. to fall silent.

"I'm not sure that Duke's as heartless and conniving as you believe him to be, A.J.," Jill said. She faced her friend squarely. "I've heard reports—some of them emotional, and I believe very credible—that to this day Duke Carrington is haunted by your brother's death and his possible part in creating that fate. He's never said an ill word against you or the Stacy family—"

"Why should he?" A.J. cried.

"Perhaps in defense of the things you've said about him."

A.J. was left feeling winded. "But I've—"

"You've been pretty brutal at times. Oh, sure, always off the record," Jill said. "But don't think it hasn't gotten back to Duke."

At the idea, A.J. felt a twisting flicker of shame, but anger and loss made her shove it away.

"Then he at least knows where I stand," A.J. said in a stiff tone. "No one can accuse me of being a hypocrite."

"I agree. But there are other labels that might fit, my dear, and some of them are not exactly what you should feel comfortable wearing."

"Such as?" A.J. baited her friend, prepared to hear her out, even if it was all for the worse.

"Just skip it," Jill said. "It would only add fuel to the Carrington-Stacy feud. I know Duke Carrington wishes that it could be ended, but I have a feeling you don't. You want to carry it to your grave."

"You'd better believe it," A.J. said, "Kip's in a grave because of Duke Carrington. That's something I'll never forget."

"And you'll never forgive it either, will you?"

A.J. gave a stubborn shake of her head, aware as she did, that she probably looked like a pouting, headstrong child.

"Then you're to be pitied even more than Duke Carrington is to be sympathized with, A.J., because you're the true loser. I know you haven't lived a perfect life. Neither have I. Without forgiveness from God—and each other—what a

bleak and hopeless existence the human condition
would be."

"Leave me alone!" A.J. choked, wadding her
napkin and bringing it to her lips as she stemmed
an angry sob.

"You're not happy, A.J., keeping alive the ani-
mosity, the anger, the blame-laying. And Duke's
not allowed to be happy, either. He's tormented.
You seem to forget that he was Kip's best friend!
I've heard it said that off the record Duke's admitted he has trouble sleeping because he made a
horrible error in judgment that cost his friend his
life. Duke doesn't have peace even now, years
later, because he knows that where he's had the
understanding and forgiveness of fans, drivers,
mechanics, race track crews—even of your father, A.J.—you're the hold out. Your blame
makes it impossible for Duke to put aside his
guilt."

"Would you lay off?"

"No! I won't. You have no family left, A.J., so
all you have is your friends. People like Beth and
like me. Well, families, my dear, are the people
who, when you go to them, have to let you in.
Friends? They're the folks who love you enough
to tell you the things that no one else would dare.
And I'm telling you that Duke Carrington wants
to buy Stacy Speedway not only as a solid business move, but so that you can make a life for
yourself, do something else, have a family and
find happiness before it's too late. He knows that
you won't, not so long as you have to worry about

Stacy Speedway. He contacted your lawyer to give you a shot at freedom and the chance to do something with it."

"My heart just bleeds," A.J. said in a sarcastic tone. "As for friends, I'm not sure you're mine. You sound like you're suddenly Duke Carrington's bosom buddy."

"Of course I'm still Duke's friend. As thick as you and I were as children, I saw a lot of Kip. Therefore, I saw more than a little of Duke. I care about you. I care about him. And I care about the Carrington family, too. I'm sure your failure to absolve him of his 'crime' has caused his wife and children untold unhappiness. People have questioned them, dragged up the painful past, and taken perverse joy in passing on the latest A.J. Stacy quote."

"I have had enough!" A.J. said, angrily rising. "I will tell you this—and it's the scoop of the day. Get a front page headline and a byline with it: The world will see A.J. Stacy dead before the speedway is sold to Duke Carrington or anyone else."

"That's just what may happen, A.J., and you're not ready to die."

"No one ever is," A.J. shot over her shoulder, and swept from Granny's Kitchen after throwing a twenty dollar bill on the counter in front of the startled cashier.

She rushed to her Corvette and squealed from the lot, racing to put as much distance as possible between her old friend and herself. Hot tears began to spill from her eyes.

In her rearview mirror, A.J. saw Jill run from the eatery, but she didn't slow down. Even when Jill desperately waved, trying to flag her down, A.J. continued on her way.

The favor that Jill had been going to propose had gone unasked. But in her heart, A.J. knew that the battle lines had been drawn. The answer was obvious to both of them.

Whatever it was, the answer was the same as would be her response to Duke Carrington's offer to buy Stacy Speedway: No!

five

After a sleepless night, A.J., feeling out of sorts and running behind, arrived at the speedway later than usual. She was pleased to see that Dan Barenfanger's midnight black Thunderbird was already in the lot.

Although she'd felt grim all morning, the prospect of seeing Dan somehow buoyed her thoughts—that is until she sternly reminded herself that he was probably married. She could already picture him putting up a family portrait in a place of prominence in the mechanic's work area.

"Hello, all!" A.J. sang out with a cheerfulness that she didn't feel.

She didn't meet Beth's eyes, nor Dan's, and she hoped that the facade of well-being would fool Beth. It had been tough enough dealing with some of the unpleasant things Jill had said. Much as she hated to admit it to herself, the facts as her friend had stated them could all too likely be true.

"Ready to get all settled in, Dan?" A.J. asked brightly.

"Yes, ma'am. I sure am," he said.

"I've been telling Dan about the wonderful things our fair city has to offer," Beth added. "Since he's unattached, I felt that he might be interested in knowing where he might meet some attractive women companions."

A.J. shot Beth a warning look. "I forgot to tell you, Dan, that Beth's an incorrigible matchmaker. When she retires, she may go into it full time and start up her own cottage business."

Dan laughed and Beth scratched her head. "That's not a bad idea, honey," she murmured.

The shrilling telephone cut off any further remarks. Beth reached for it, listened, then waved A.J. and Dan away as she attended to a brief business call.

"If anyone phones for me while I'm showing Dan around," A.J. called over her shoulder, "either page me on the intercom so I can take it at the closest phone or take a message and I'll give the party a callback."

"Will do," Beth said.

"Ready to go survey your kingdom?" A.J. invited Dan.

"Looking forward to it like a kid anticipating Christmas."

"Super!" A.J. said and felt her spirits lift even more. Simply being with Dan seemed to make her feel an inescapable and unexplainable happiness.

"After all these years, it's going to be wonderful to be associated with an Indy-bound driver again."

Slowly they made their way around the Stacy Speedway complex. A.J. told Dan everything he needed to know, and even a few things that weren't absolutely necessary. He seemed enthralled by the funny, poignant stories she told from the past.

"I think you'll be very happy here," A.J. concluded when she had finished giving Dan Barenfanger the grand tour.

"I know that I will be," he agreed.

"Get caught up in the mechanical area, and then we can worry about what you can do to take some of the pressure off me on the managerial side. I don't want to overload you, Dan."

"I appreciate it," he said. "After all, I am only human—even though Beth Carter led me to believe that you viewed me as something more than a mere mortal."

"She told you that?"

"Yes. I'm sorry to repeat it if it's not quite true," Dan apologized awkwardly, "or if it's not exactly what you said."

"Don't be, Dan," A.J. said. "That's the gist of what I did say. But let it be a warning to both of us that our dear Beth Carter will be giving her all in hopes of arranging for us to mix business and pleasure."

"Forewarned is forearmed," Dan agreed seriously, and in such a way that suddenly A.J. felt unattractive. She wondered for a moment if he was agreeing so readily because he did not find her desirable or appealing.

"I'll see you later," A.J. said limply and quickly left.

Beth, her eyes twinkling, was on the telephone

when A.J. returned to the office. A.J. knew just by observing the way Beth laughed and nodded her head that she was talking to a personal friend. Beth quickly brought the call to a conclusion.

"Any calls while I was out?" A.J. asked.

"A few, hon. Those I couldn't handle on your behalf are lined up in order on Post-It Notes on your desk."

"Great. I'll get right to work. We won't have much time to ourselves until the weekend stock car events are over."

"We've got a full slate of entrants booked."

"The accountant will be overjoyed to learn of that," A.J. said, and Beth laughed.

"Are you going out for lunch?" Beth asked quietly.

A.J. looked up quickly. "Now why would you want to know that?" she asked, perplexed. "You've never really cared before."

"Oh, I . . . uh . . . I thought. Never mind," Beth said, and seemed relieved when the telephone rang again. A.J. disappeared into her private office area.

She attacked the documents that had come in the morning mail, endorsed the checks that Beth had neatly prepared for her signature, and set them with appropriate invoices for Beth to post.

Before A.J. realized it, the radio had carried the scheduled thirty-second spots advertising the weekend stock car racing events and the noon market reporters were airing their news.

She considered ordering something from a fast-food restaurant nearby and sending Beth to bring back lunch for all of them, but the sound of a car pulling into the parking lot momentarily diverted her attention. An instant later she stared in shock as a familiar car came in view and nosed into the space between her Corvette and Dan's Thunderbird.

Jill!

Memories from the unpleasant encounter in Granny's Kitchen the night before fast-forwarded to front and center in A.J.'s mind. She felt anger boil to the surface again.

"Well, Jill," Beth trilled, "what a surprise!"

From the tone of their voices, A.J. realized that Beth had been expecting her friend. Suddenly the older woman's undue interest in A.J.'s luncheon plans was easily explained.

"A.J. around?" Jill asked pleasantly.

"In her office. Go on in."

A moment later, Jill appeared at A.J.'s office door. "Should I throw my hat through the door first?"

"Come on in," A.J. invited.

Jill did, bringing with her a large, white package with orange trim. Wonderful scents exuded from it.

"I stopped at the florist's," Jill said, "and they were fresh out of the olive branch of peace. Will a sixteen inch pepperoni pizza do?"

"Pizza or no pizza, Jill, I couldn't have stayed mad at you. I'm afraid I'm the one who owes the apology."

"It takes two to tangle."

"Would three make it a crowd?" Beth asked, sniffing deeply, then twitching her nose like a rabbit. The woman burst into laughter as they hauled Beth into the room, positioned her in A.J.'s vacated chair, and served her the first piece of piping hot pizza.

"Mmmmm, this is delicious," A.J. said. "I don't know if we'll get it all eaten before you have to return to the paper."

Jill swallowed a quick bite. "I've got all afternoon. I took the rest of the day off."

"Yeah?"

"I cited personal problems."

"Me?" A.J. asked. "You're that concerned?"

"I never did get to ask my favor."

"After last night, I didn't think you'd want anything from me."

"I still want that favor from you. And I want a whole lot of happiness for you as well."

"My, but this is a lot of pizza," Beth commented.

"Why don't you give Dan a call over the intercom," A.J. suggested, "and invite him to eat with us. I wish I'd have thought of it earlier. I'm not used to having a mechanic around again."

"Oh, honey, I'm too stuffed to move. Would you call him?"

"I guess," A.J. said, "but don't you dare read into this action any more than is actually there."

"And that's?" Jill prompted.

"An invitation to an employee. Nothing more,

nothing less."

A.J. extended the invitation and Dan quickly accepted. The four enjoyed each other's company, and it was with reluctance that Beth went back to her work area and Dan returned to the shop. Jill stayed to have a few minutes of private conversation with her friend.

"He's a really nice guy, isn't he?"

"I think so. But I don't really know. He only started working here this morning."

"No kidding? Then you, Amanda Jane Stacy, are what is known as a fast worker. That guy was looking at you with rather worshipful glances."

A.J. groaned. "Been talking to Beth, have you?"

"As a matter of fact, no. I have the instincts of an ace reporter, remember? I've been trained to observe carefully and look for nuances in what's said and done."

"Okay. I like Dan. Dan seems to like me. Aside from that I'm afraid I have no comment."

"Well, with him around, A.J., I can see why you're not in any hurry to sell the speedway."

"Jill, this hasn't been a good topic for us."

"Maybe you're meant to sell the speedway, A.J."

"Jill, up until this moment, the visit has been wonderful. Please don't undo what ground we regained over the pepperoni pizza-of-peace."

"Then at the risk of doing just that, I will continue, my friend. I feel that it's time I said my piece."

"If I recall correctly, you did that last night."

"On one level of discussion, yes. Today I want to break some fresh ground. I want to talk to you about the purpose to be found in your life. Will you hear me out?"

A dubious A.J. nodded reluctant agreement.

What she had been expecting was not what she got. Instead of hearing a lecture, A.J. listened to Jill talk about how she'd met Rod. She described how all the events beautifully fell together. With the clarity of retrospect, Jill could see how her entire life had seemed to lead toward that moment.

"I know that Rod and I are meant to marry," Jill said, "and that we'll find fulfillment with each other. Together, we'll more perfectly discover the divine purpose for our lives. You have a God-given purpose to your existence, too, A.J., and it's up to you to find it by seeking His will instead of stubbornly pursuing your own obsessive desires. Have you ever given that any thought? What do you feel about that?"

"I . . . uh." Feeling put on the spot, A.J. flushed.

Jill chuckled. "You don't have to try to soothe my feelings. You probably think I've fallen over the deep end, right? Well, just know that I used to think I was really a together-type person. I used to get nervous when I was around people who talked about God as if He were someone real, like you and I are, and not some phantomlike, philosophical, abstract, unapproachable entity.

Since I've come to know the Lord on a personal basis, A.J., now I know where it's really at. And I want others to have that too. Especially you, a lifelong friend."

"When did this happen?" A.J. asked, startled.

"It wasn't an overnight transformation," Jill explained. "You know me. 'Skeptic' could have been my middle name. And you know how reporters are about digging for the facts themselves."

"Right," A.J. agreed, breathing a bit easier.

"Soon after I met Rod, I realized that he was a committed Christian who wasn't apologizing for it and who unashamedly studied the Bible. I decided to see what this worshipful Christian devotion was all about. I got out a Bible that I hadn't opened in years, and I started reading. It was as if I were seeing it anew."

"But I thought you'd read through the Bible several years ago when you were in college."

Jill nodded. "I did. A four-credit course entitled, 'The Bible as Literature.' It was delivered by a boring professor who was either an atheist or at best an agnostic. Studying Scripture both on my own and with knowledgeable Christians and a good commentary and concordance, I've reached a lot of fresh conclusions in areas where before my mind was foolishly closed."

"Such as?"

"That there's a Redeemer, A.J., a God-Man who died for me. A God who died for you. A Lord and Savior who cares about me. But He also is very concerned about you, A.J., and is aware of every jot and tittle of your daily life, your past, your future."

"How nice," A.J. murmured when silence sprang between them and seemed to beg for a comment. Her words sounded flat and artificial even to her own ears. "This is certainly a far cry from your sophisticated college girl views."

"I thank God for that," Jill sighed.

"You know," A.J. said, and carefully changed the subject, "that's one thing that I really regret. That I didn't go off to college. Dad offered to send me when you went away to the university. But I chose to hang around the speedway being Beth's pain-in-the-neck Girl Friday."

"You stayed at the speedway because it was comfortable. There was no challenge. You knew what to expect. University and a future with a career other than racing were frightening unknowns. Challenges. Risks."

"I suppose," A.J. sighed.

"Less of a risk than roaring around the racetrack in a souped-up stock car at the speed of light, my dear."

"I'm not so sure I can agree with you on that one, Jill. Behind the wheel of a car, I know what I'm doing. And in the college classroom, I wouldn't. Anyway, this is all rhetorical. It's too late now. I made my choice. Now I have to live with it."

"That's where you're wrong. It's never too late. Why, if you wanted to give it a whirl, you

could go evenings. Or get someone like Dan to
take over so you could go during the days. Who
knows, A.J., you could end up embarking on a
whole new career."

"And wouldn't Duke Carrington love that?"
A.J. asked in a dry tone. She looked at Jill. "Is he
paying you a commission?"

"What kind of remark is that?"

"An ugly one," A.J. said. "I'm sorry. It's just
that—"

"Just that you're as obsessed with Duke
Carrington as you are obsessed with the Indy
500. Maybe it's time to give it a rest, A.J. Why
not give it up?"

"It's not an obsession! It's my dream. And I
will not give it up. I'll get to the Indy or die
trying."

"A.J., that's what I'm afraid of." Jill's eyes
suddenly filled with tears. "I'm an old family
friend, remember? We've lost Kip. Your dad.
And now you're intent on following the same
path they took. We're concerned."

"We this, we that, we everything. Who's this
'we' you're talking about?"

"I protect my sources, A.J.," Jill said in a level
tone. "So that's for me to know, you to find out,
and I'll never tell."

"Mother?"

"I said I don't reveal my sources. You're still
not on speaking terms with your mother?"

A.J. gave a curt shake of her head. "Gift
exchanges for birthdays and Christmas, but

that's it."

"That's better than no contact at all. You don't see much hope for a reconciliation?"

A.J. gave a bitter laugh. " 'Fraid not, Pollyanna. She's obsessed with the idea that I give up racing."

Jill shrugged. "No more obsessed than you are with staying in the race. The Indy 500 and the speedway are more important to you than your mother? More important than going to college and finding fulfillment in a career? More important than finding Mr. Right, marrying, and having a family of your own? So all-fired important—this dream, this goal, this obsession that you refuse to call by its real name—that you'll die for it?"

"Yes!"

"Then you're to be pitied, A.J., and prayed for. I trust that God will provide you mercy and the time you need. Then you can recognize your crippling hang-ups and discover the truth before you no longer are able to set meaningful priorities in life."

"Oh, like you? Marrying some man, being content to leave a promising position and start all over again in a new city?" A.J. said, finding herself sneering, even as she hated herself for doing so.

"Speaking of which, there's something—"

A.J. held up her hand. "Don't ask now, Jill," she whispered, "because neither of us would like the answer. I'm sorry, but that's the way it is."

"Okay," Jill said. "I'll abide by that." She gave A.J.'s shoulder a fond pat. "No hard feelings," she clarified, and added with a note of finality, "and I will see you later."

six

Two days passed.

Over the weekend, A.J. was too busy with the speedway's regular competition to give personal cares a moment's attention. But when the last spectator had driven away, the sanitation service has policed the grounds, and only Beth's car, Dan's, and her own were in front of the office complex, A.J. had time to give Jill's words some thought. The more she considered their conversation, the more incensed she became.

Beth was unusually quiet in her disapproval, and A.J. felt like railing at her, too, for she suspected that Beth and Jill had been in touch with each other—on their own time, of course. The notion of them plotting against her, a couple of Christians who were thick as thieves, almost drove her to distraction.

When Dan unintentionally commented on Jill's pizza surprise, he provided A.J. the catalyst she needed to release her tightly suppressed emotions.

"Jill used to be my very best friend, Dan," she erupted. "Now she makes me so mad I can hardly see straight."

"Why's that?" he asked as he soaked parts in gasoline, cleaned them off, and toweled them dry.

"Oh, I don't know," A.J. grumped. "Now that she's engaged to be married it's like she's queen of the world and has all the answers or something. She has a clear view of where she's going, and she acts like she has a detailed vision of where I'm meant to go, too.

"Maybe all women who get engaged are like that," A.J. added as an afterthought. "I wouldn't know. How about you?"

"How about me what?" Dan asked, apparently focusing on refitting, adjusting, and securing the newly cleaned parts.

"Do you know anything about engaged women?"

" 'Fraid not," he said. "When my older sister got engaged, I was too young to be very observant."

"You've never been engaged?"

"Uh-uh."

"Hmmm."

For a moment, A.J.'s surly mood lifted. She'd already known from Beth's light remark that Dan was unmarried, but she had been too proud to ask if this was because he had been separated, divorced, widowed, or never married at all. She supposed that she could have checked his file for herself, but she was afraid that Beth might have laid a trap for her to reveal her interest in Dan—something like a hair stretched across the file folder, giving her away if it was dislodged.

"Jill's also been driving me crazy because she's got a pipeline to some gossip source about the speedway," A.J. went on, standing beside Dan and automatically cleaning parts to hand to him as he needed them. "I think she knows more than she's telling me. There is gossip and rumors are going around."

Suddenly A.J. had Dan's undivided attention. He stared at her, his troubled gaze searching her face.

"Like what?"

"Like I don't know for sure. Except that someone would like to buy Stacy Speedway."

"That's not that big a thing," Dan said and went back to work. "I'm sure that's common for anyone who owns a going business concern."

"I suppose so," A.J. said. "But what scares me is that there are ways people who want to take over a business can succeed by using hostile techniques. Even a flourishing business like Stacy Speedway could end up forced to sell through chicanery."

"What do you mean?"

"Even though it sounds paranoid," A.J. said, "I worry about rigging. Some driver creating an accident resulting in the speedway being found liable and getting sued to the max. Or even more far out, what if there was something being done to make things go bad from the inside out?"

"I'm afraid you lost me there, girl. What are you driving at?"

"Something akin to a racetrack blockbuster."

"You're still not getting through to me, A.J."

"In big cities, Dan, sometimes a landlord of a building will be in a rent-controlled situation. He can't raise the rent on the building, and he can't evict people so that the new tenants can be charged the higher rent. If the building is razed and a new one put up, then they can charge what they want because the old rules won't apply and—"

A.J. felt frustrated. "Don't you see what I'm driving at? If a blockbuster can go in and clean out a building, perhaps someone close to me could be convinced to—"

Dan let out a startled whistle. "Now I get what you're driving at. At least I think I do. You're starting to believe that Jill Alexander has been hired to convince you to sell Stacy Speedway? Giving you all the advice as a loving friend?"

"Yes. While consorting with the enemy, who happens to be her long-time friend, too."

"And who's that?" Dan asked.

"Duke Carrington."

At the mention of the man A.J. held responsible for Kip's death, the mechanic's face grew strained. When she explained her deep-seated emotions, Dan's face grew ashen.

"I can appreciate how you feel, A.J.," Dan said softly. "But you're hurting A.J. Stacy far more than you're injuring Duke Carrington. You're not going to like it, but I have to cast my lot with Beth, with Jill, and probably with a whole lot of others. I think it's time for you to forgive Duke Carrington."

"What are you? Just one more in my intimate circle of traitors?"

"No, A.J. Simply one more committed Christian who cares."

"You, too?" A.J. cried. She began to swipe at angry tears. "I thought you Christians were supposed to be so nice, that you were supposed to go around comforting people, not making them feel so confused and caught between contradicting, conflicting choices."

"Sometimes we comfort, A.J.," Dan admitted. "And sometimes we challenge. But don't forget that we always care." He put his arm around her shoulder and gave her a quick, companionable hug.

"Thanks. And I'm sorry if I said things that were insulting or suspicious."

"It's okay. I know you didn't mean them."

"I really didn't. I've been so confused lately. And afraid. I'm just not myself at times."

"I know that without being told. But the one who needs to hear your explanations and apology is Jill."

"I've been a cross for her to bear."

"She'll forgive you."

"I know she will. Maybe at one time she wouldn't have, but this new Jill will."

"What time's it getting to be?" Dan asked.

"Quitting time."

"Here and at the *Daily News*," he pointed out.

A.J. gave a weak laugh. It seemed like her first in a week. "And what's that supposed to mean?"

"I thought that I might take two gorgeous girls out to supper," Dan said in a casual tone. "I have something special in mind. Pepperoni peace pizza."

"Put on olives," A.J. said.

"Hold the branches," Dan whispered.

"In case you are interested in Jill, I guess you did know that Jill is taken?"

"You mentioned that when you were feeling considerably more irate a few minutes ago."

A.J. blushed at the memory. She hadn't been very nice and she was ashamed of herself, but she sensed that Dan knew that without being told. He seemed to look beyond the human hurt to the woman who still cared.

"So I did, didn't I?" she asked in a light tone.

Dan extended his hand, and A.J. accepted his warm grip. "But you're not," he clarified. "So what do you say we make arrangements to get together with Jill? Being as you're her girlfriend of such longstanding, I have a hunch there's something she's been meaning to ask you. Tonight, be a good girl and give her the chance, huh?"

"I'll try," A.J. said and felt a special thrill when he squeezed her hand.

"If you feel like you're going to explode, just say a quick prayer and ask God to handle your temper. He can control the things that are too big for us to handle."

"Like love?" A.J. wanted to ask. She was surprised by a sudden desire to slip into his arms, to feel them around her as she savored his gentle lips on hers.

Like hate?

The warm thoughts of love were replaced by an ice cold specter of dislike, distrust, and blame. A myriad of negative emotions closed like cold tentacles to strangle the shoot of hope that had blossomed in her heart.

"You name it," Dan assured, as if he could read her mind, "and the Lord God can attend to it."

"I hope so," she whispered.

And truly she did for she felt herself quickly beginning to fall in love with Dan Barenfanger, as swiftly and completely as one shattering moment had caused her to begin despising Duke Carrington.

Duke.

She couldn't even remember what his real name was. David? Donald? At one time she'd known, not that it was important now.

She felt a sudden jolt when she realized that while her hatred of Duke still glowed bright within her breast—a cancerous, killing thing—she couldn't bring to mind a current picture of him. The best she could do was the picture snapped by some sportswriter, a ghoulish candid shot, showing Kip's shrouded body being carted away on the ambulance stretcher, while a broken Duke Carrington's face crumpled in agonized tears.

And the only way she could replace that mental picture was by calling up images from a bygone era when the Carringtons and the Stacys had been the state's racing families supreme. When people speculated that one day a wedding would bond the lineage of the racing lineups forever.

It was a romantic merger that had never come to pass.

And from a corner of her mind came A.J.'s

maverick thought. She was tired, oh so tired, that
it would be almost a relief to sell Stacy Speedway,
give over the dream to Duke Carrington, bury the
past as she'd buried her family, and get on with
facing the future and discovering the true purpose
behind A.J. Stacy's existence.

seven

Dan held the office door open for A.J. to exit, pulled it firmly closed behind them, and waited for her to lock up.

"Instead of taking two cars, I'll drive my Thunderbird and bring you back here later," he offered. "I have a few things I want to attend to in the shop."

"Super," A.J. agreed. "I have several odds and ends to take care of in the office."

"If we hurry, we should get to the pizza place at the same time Jill will," he said as he unlocked his car and held the door for A.J. to slide in.

Fifteen minutes later, Dan parked in the lot of the pizzeria and Jill squeezed her car in beside his. A.J. and Dan waited for the reporter to exit her car, then Dan gallantly offered each girl an arm.

"I was so relieved when you called me at the *News*," Jill said.

"I can't stay mad at you," A.J. admitted.

"And I can't bear it when you are. I guess you know that you've ruined my telephone bill this week. I've been calling Rod almost every night to cry on his shoulder about you."

A.J. felt herself stiffen. "Really?" she murmured in a light tone, not at all sure that she was comfortable with the situation.

The way Dan gave her a quick look, A.J. was aware that he'd felt her arm tighten against his.

"I felt better after Rod and I talked," Jill said.

A.J. tried not to feel nettled, as she reminded herself that Rod was going to be Jill's husband. It stood to reason that she'd turn to him for comfort and consolation before going to others.

"Rod said he'd have his Christian businessmen's breakfast club pray for you at their weekly prayer meeting. They'll pray that if you're meant to face a career change, you'll make the right decision. There's real power in prayer, you know."

A.J. didn't, and she felt the odd resentments build. From the heat warming her cheeks, she could detect that her temper was rising. When she felt a soft nudge against her foot after they were seated, she knew that Dan had noticed her unusually high color. She recalled what he'd said about praying to God to handle her temper so another evening wouldn't be shattered.

When A.J. thought it through, she almost laughed. She was struck by how illogical it seemed to take refuge in prayer when she was upset and vulnerable and defensive just because so many people—rank strangers—were praying on her behalf. Did they think she was some kind of social incompetent whose actions were running out of control?

Dan's smile was almost conspiratorial as if he, too, saw and recognized A.J.'s inner feelings and understood the amusing ironies. But it was also obvious that he was treating her feelings with respect.

Any of the irritations that might have surfaced evaporated when from beneath the red and white checkered vinyl table cloth Dan's hand protectively sought A.J.'s. Suddenly, at the warm, gentle, caring contact, she was overwhelmed with a feeling of joy and belonging. At that moment it seemed as if everything had been put right in her world. A.J. wanted to spread such happiness around by making it a memorable meal.

The waitress set their soft drinks in front of her three hungry customers and promised that the pepperoni pizza—with olives—would be ready soon.

"It seems to me that I recall you have a favor that you wanted to ask me," A.J. prompted. "I'm all ears, if you still want to ask. And if you've changed your mind, I'll understand."

"Great minds travel the same ruts," Jill chuckled. "A.J., that was just what was on the tip of my tongue. Anyway, Rod and I want you to be maid of honor at our wedding. Will you? Please?"

"Oh, Jill—with pleasure!"

Jill glowed with relief and happiness.

"I felt certain you would. At least I hoped you would. You're the girl closest to me. I'm so glad you're agreeable. That's one less detail to worry about."

"When is the big day?"

"Not for quite a while," Jill admitted. "Next winter. We're planning a December wedding. We'll be using Christmas colors."

"It'll be beautiful."

"I've been looking at red dresses for my attendants," Jill said. "With your dark hair you should be a knockout in red. We're thinking about holly sprigs and short veils for the attendants, too, and perhaps white velvet muffs with a red rose."

"Sounds lovely," A.J. said. "Don't you think so, Dan?"

"Very nice."

"You'll be invited too, Dan, if you want to come," Jill happily planned. "Nothing's set in stone. We've got a lot of time."

"But there's a lot to get done," A.J. pointed out.

"You're right. December will be here before we know it. Rod and I are hoping that the contractor will have our house done by then so it'll be ready to move in. They'll be pouring the basement next week. And framing it up soon after that."

"Jill, this is so exciting. You must be in seventh heaven."

"Hardly a cloud on the horizon, although my lease expires mid-October. I'll store most of my belongings into our new house then, and I can probably live at a hotel paying buy-the-week rates until I leave the *Daily News* and move away."

"You'll do nothing of the sort," A.J. insisted. "You can stay with me at my apartment."

"You're sure?"

"If I had doubts, I wouldn't be offering the invitation."

"Well, that's another problem solved. One less thing to worry about."

"Pizza is served!" Dan announced as the waitress came to them carrying a huge pie and a pitcher of cola. "Eat up!"

A.J. could have purred with content when Dan helped her into his Thunderbird later that evening. The three friends had lingered for hours over their meal, talking.

"Tonight was great, Dan. I enjoyed it, and I know that Jill did, too. It was sweet of you to suggest this so that Jill and I could get things straightened out."

"I enjoyed it, too," he admitted.

"I don't think I could have eaten another bite," A.J. said. "Now I'm so satiated and warm I could take a nap over that work that's waiting for me in the office."

"I have a coffee pot in the shop. I could brew some java to help revive your senses."

"I've got an urn in the office, too. Care for a cup when we get to the speedway—before we both get back to the business at hand?"

"You're on," Dan agreed in an easy tone.

Talk between them was comfortable when they returned to the quiet office. A.J. fixed coffee, then turned on the radio, tuning to an easy-listening station.

With the piping hot coffee, she felt the sluggishness leave her system, and she grew more alert and ready to tackle her paperwork.

Dan glanced at his wristwatch. "I'd better get to the shop, get my work done, and turn in for the night."

"Yeah, me, too," A.J. said.

As Dan prepared to leave, for no real reason that she could later figure out, A.J. walked with him. They stepped outside into the chilly dark night, making small talk and laughing in a companionable manner.

She found herself repeating heartfelt thanks for a wonderful evening, and she noticed that Dan seemed to be hesitating, reluctant to leave. Suddenly she was very aware of him as a handsome man, and from the look in his eyes, she knew that he was not immune to the fact that she was an attractive woman.

She wasn't sure if she moved toward him or if he drew her into his embrace, but the next thing she knew, his arms slipped tenderly around her, drew her close, and his lips dropped to hers for a thrilling, sweetly pleasant kiss.

Then, a moment later, his lips that had teased hers, soft as a butterfly's wing, were removed, leaving her feeling cheated when the precious contact was gone.

"Goodnight," he whispered. "Stay sweet."

Then, as if he could not help himself, he dropped another quick caress to her lips, turned, and walked away. A.J. stood shivering in the chilly night, though Dan's quick expression of affection had warmed her to the bone.

She let herself back into her office, but it was impossible to work. She'd been kissed before—many times—but never as satisfyingly as when Dan Barenfanger's lips had fleetingly made such loving contact with hers.

Finally, after she'd heard his Thunderbird leave the lot, A.J. locked up the office and left the compound, her Corvette streaking through the night to her apartment.

As soon as she reached home, A.J. showered and slipped into a soft flannel gown. Admittedly, she was tired, but she couldn't fall asleep no matter how she tried. The image of Dan Barenfanger and the perfection of his kisses kept her awake until almost the dawning of a brand new day.

Even though A.J. was dreadfully tired the next morning, she was up at her customary hour and found herself humming as she dressed with more than her usual care. She was being fastidious about her makeup, and she realized it was because she was anticipating seeing Dan.

She arrived at the speedway a few minutes before she usually got to the office building, and Dan was already there. Her heart skipped a beat in anticipation of seeing him, but when she let herself into the office, he greeted her with the same cordiality that he presented Beth Carter. No more, no less.

A.J. had expected some kind of reaction from him, a gesture or a word to signify that he acknowledged the previous evening's kiss. She felt disappointed when he seemed to ignore the event.

A moment later, she comforted herself that he was simply being discreet in front of Beth, who they both knew was something of a matchmaker.

But the day and then the week wore on. Dan made no mention of their encounter, and he treated A.J. in a circumspectly businesslike manner. Gradually she realized that he was intent on distancing himself from her.

In her hurt and pride she, too, grew more aloof.

By the time two months had passed, A.J. appeared to have forgotten the thrilling kisses she'd exchanged with Dan as thoroughly as had he. And she'd gained control of her emotions to the point where she believed that she could talk about Dan without revealing to Beth what her true feelings were.

"How'd your church potluck turn out last night, Beth?" A.J. asked one Monday morning following a beautiful spring weekend.

"Marvelous," Beth said, "it couldn't have been nicer."

"Anyone there I know?" A.J. asked.

Beth ran through a list of names. "And Dan, of course."

"He's making friends in the community," A.J.

stated. "I think that's nice." She took a quick breath and hoped her tone didn't betray her feelings. "Is he going with anyone yet?"

"Not that I'm aware of," Beth said. "I guess we keep him too busy at the speedway."

"That's his own fault," A.J. said. "I let him set his own hours. I'm hardly such a slave-driver that he can't have an evening free to pursue other interests."

"I'm afraid he's like you, honey, and race cars are his interest. He'd sooner tear down an engine and rebuild it, or fool around with a thirteen-speed transmission, than make the acquaintance of some nice girl."

"I'll bet some of them at your church are interested in him, too, aren't they?"

"Why I should hope to tell you that they are," Beth said in an enthusiastic tone. "And while he's nice to them, he certainly doesn't offer any girl any encouragement."

"That's sort of strange, isn't it?" A.J. murmured. "At his age, you'd think he'd have been serious about some woman. Or have already been married. What's wrong with him?"

"Nothing," Beth said. "He simply hasn't met the right girl yet. At least that's what he said."

"You've actually asked him about his love life, Beth? Or rather, his lack of one?"

"The topic's come up a time or two," she admitted in an innocent tone. "Someday he'll get married. There are a lot of girls who are attractive to him, but Dan Barenfanger is a truly discerning man. It'll take more than a pretty face and knock-out figure to gain Dan's attention and devotion. He's simply never found the right Christian girl yet, so he says."

A.J.'s heart felt like it stopped beating.

Of course, she thought, as her pulse slowed almost to a death knell cadence with disappointment. She considered what Jill had had to say about shared faith. She knew Beth's beliefs on the matter. So it should have gone without saying that Dan Barenfanger, who was a committed Christian, would seek the same from any woman he'd consider for a wife.

"That's sort of limiting himself, isn't it?" A.J. spoke her thoughts but wished a moment later that she hadn't.

"Pardon me?" Beth replied, obviously having lost the thread of their conversation.

"What I said is that Dan's rather limiting himself by not going out with girls who aren't what you people refer to as committed Christians, isn't he? He could be denying himself some wonderful friendships."

"Ummm, perhaps. But there are several ways of looking at that, A.J. Sure, he could be denying himself some wonderful women friends, but he could also be sparing people heartbreak. It's not wise to be unequally yoked, you know, and how sad it is if people who are so unsuited for one another should fall in love and marry and be pulling in opposite directions all the time."

"Yes, but—"

"You don't miss what you've never had, A.J. And if Dan misses out on some delightful unbeliever, he may be sparing himself—and the young woman—a lot of unpleasantness and tension and turmoil."

"It seems such a callous, calculating attitude."

"I can see where it might seem that way to some people, but I understand it perfectly. Dan's trusting in God to bring the woman meant for him into his life. So with faith in God to provide in love as well as provide in life, Dan can attend to business and know that he's pursuing the will of God. If he were out beating the bushes looking for women to date, he could end up overlooking the very girl that the Lord wanted to reveal to him."

"Jill talks about Christianity being such a logical, simple way of life," A.J. said. "But it sure sounds complicated to me."

"Not when the Lord opens your eyes, your ears, and your heart to His message. Then what seems foolish to the unbeliever becomes the most precious wisdom to the man or woman made new in the Lord."

"Well," A.J. said in a breezy tone, as if it were none of her concern what Dan did with his spare time. "I won't feel so guilty usurping Dan's time now that we're heading into prime racing season. At least when he's on the road with me to head up the pit crew, I won't feel guilty about taking him away from a woman he loves."

"And he'll have an enjoyable time," Beth assured, "because he cares about you as much as he does any woman. So until our Dan Barenfanger meets Miss Right—enjoy, A.J., enjoy!"

eight

That summer, A.J. Stacy got her racing career back on track.

Commitments of time proved more demanding than she and Dan had realized and turned out to be pushing the edge of what they were able to manage.

"I don't know what we're going to do," A.J. said as she stared at the speedway calendar and then at the professional racing schedule for the upcoming months. "It's impossible to be two places at one time. So far we've lucked out, Dan. But the good fortune isn't holding. I don't want to miss some of the big races. And it would be disastrous to try to change the dates we've already scheduled here at the speedway. The confusion could create a financial debacle."

"I know," Dan commiserated.

"I need you with me, and yet the speedway requires your presence here. There's no alternative," A.J. said. "We'll simply have to hire a track manager."

She sighed heavily.

Dan made a wry face.

"The accountant ought to just love that idea," he said in a droll tone.

Already Dan Barenfanger had crossed swords with the slight, bookish, older gentleman who was a whiz with figures and overhead cost analysis, as well as a genius in his number crunching abilities. The accountant guarded Stacy Speedway profits as if they were his own.

A.J. gave a weary snort.

"I have half a notion to fire him and get an accountant who gives me less grief. But any time I even think about that option, Beth argues against it. I believe she'd have a stroke on the spot if I changed accountants. She's worked with the firm for years; they're the only people she'll let touch her tax papers. Her trust is implicit."

Dan shrugged. "The man is only doing his job, A.J.," he pointed out.

A.J. nodded. "Yes. If at times, insufferably so."

"You've got to admit—his input and suggested strictures have helped you amass the funds to finance you for the Indy. Without him, you probably couldn't have done it."

"And Dad trusted him as much, or even more, than Beth," A.J. recalled. "But for crying out loud, Dan, there's got to be a solution somewhere. In someone."

"We can pray for the answers to make it all work."

A.J. turned away from him, rolling her eyes.

"We can also hope that no more major races conflict with prime dates on the speedway's calendar."

"If they do, then don't cancel your plans to compete. I have faith that something will work out."

Dan had such an element of certainty in his tone that A.J. gave him a quick look. "Is there something you're aware of that I don't know about?"

"Only that Beth's working on it with her prayer partners," Dan admitted. "And Jill and Rod, too. I've been pestering the Lord about it more than a little bit, as well."

A.J. shook her head in disbelief.

"Then I must be the only person who's not praying for miracle solutions. Instead I keep myself busy looking for viable options."

Rather than rise to the bait, Dan merely seemed to shrug it off and changed the subject by bringing their conversation around to the upcoming race four hundred miles away.

"We squeaked by this time," he said. "If all goes well, we can conclude the speedway's stock events and immediately hit the road with the racer and arrive in time for you to drive."

"Yes, we could," A.J. said thoughtfully, feeling better. "Tell you what. I'll help out in the shop so we can have the racer loaded, everything in order, and be ready to roll almost as soon as the last heat's done."

"Good enough. It'll work out. Somehow it always does," Dan said confidently.

"This time, yes," A.J. sighed. Then her tone grew bleak. "But what about next time?"

"We'll worry about that when we face it."

During the next week, A.J.'s days were long and her nights were even longer. When she finished her office work, she often joined Dan in the shop, prepared to assist him.

"We're going to come in ahead of schedule," he assured her.

"Good," she said, "because the speedway's business and routine will be demanding your managerial duties when the crowds get here to watch the stock car competition."

"We're going to meet ourselves coming and going."

"Dan, seriously, I think I'm going to put out feelers to see about hiring a race track manager. It's inevitable. So I may as well bite the bullet and do it."

"Instead do me a favor, A.J. Give us another week, okay? If we don't have a workable solution by then, I'll be the first to agree that we should get a full-time manager."

"When all we really need is part time," she mused.

"Or better yet, even free lance," he revised accordingly.

A.J. groaned at the perfection of that idea, then gave a disbelieving laugh.

"Dream on, dreamer," she invited.

"With God all things are possible," Dan reminded in a soft tone.

"Possible, yes. Probable, no," was A.J.'s parting shot.

nine

"Business at the speedway was brisk today," Dan said after he shifted gears and eased the large transport that bore A.J.'s racer onto the interstate entrance ramp.

"The ticket office had tabbed receipts and today was the season's all-time high so far."

"Great. Concession stand workers seemed to be kept busy, too."

"It's been a first rate day. Let's hope our luck holds, Dan."

"My most fervent prayer."

"While you're at it, you may as well throw in one for me and the race. Being as it's a major one."

"I already have, A.J." Dan shot her a sideways glance. "What's the matter? You nervous?"

A.J. nodded. "I shouldn't be. But I am."

"Why?"

"This is the first time in quite a while that I've really come up against the big guys."

"But you're one of them, A.J. You're going to be the Indy Girl, remember? You can hold your own. You can drive with the best of them. There's nothing and no one to get psyched out over."

It was on the tip of A.J.'s tongue to admit that indeed there was and his name was Duke Carrington. But she managed to control herself and contain the worried-sounding admission.

A.J. had been optimistically anticipating the big race, viewing it as a chance to see longtime friends she hadn't encountered for quite a while. But her good feelings quickly evaporated and were replaced by negative emotions when she had learned that among her competitors was veteran driving ace Duke Carrington. He had either won or placed in any race worth entering.

A.J. dreaded confronting Duke, even as she knew that she would have to. She wasn't overly upset at facing off professionally, but she was concerned about a personal confrontation. And she was also worried about the sensitivities of their mutual friends who might feel caught in the middle of a continuing conflict.

For the past several years, avoidance was how A.J. had coped. But now there was no remaining on the fringes. She couldn't let Duke Carrington stand between her and the Indy 500.

"You ought to see a lot of friends, huh?" Dan asked, breaking the silence and seeming to read A.J.'s thoughts.

"More than just a few. You too?"

"Uh-huh. I'm looking forward to it. Some of us used to hang pretty tight. But that was a long time ago. Back when I was driving instead of standing by in the pit."

"How come you quit driving, Dan?"

He paused. "It's a long story."

A.J. glanced at her watch. "It's a long drive ahead of us."

"You might think that I'm preaching at you, A.J.,

because in order to answer your question I'd have to explain my motivations. I know how you feel about people who trust in the Creator, who believe that there are answers to be found from outside themselves." He paused and gave A.J. an assessing glance. There was a twinkle in his eye, but a dubious expression on his face. "Are you sure that you want to hear the story of my life?"

"I'll risk it," A.J. said. "Do tell."

Dan was silent several minutes. At first A.J. thought he'd changed his mind about sharing a story from the past. But then she realized that he was merely collecting his thoughts. His voice was soft and reflective as he began to talk about how he'd been entranced by motors even when he was a child.

"I was constantly dinging around with engines," Dan explained. "Even as a kid not much more than knee high, I could take apart a lawn-mower engine and make it work."

"And you were the most popular little boy in the neighborhood, right?"

Dan grinned. "You've got that right. There were several widow ladies on our block. I kept their mowers purring like pussycats. Then I graduated to bigger gas engines when I got into school. I was fortunate in that our district had a vocational setup in the classroom. I learned everything that we had to study in the classroom environment, and the instructor challenged me by giving me extra credit assignments."

"Bet you pulled some easy A's, huh?"

"A's yes, but not easily at all," Dan clarified.

A.J. realized that a number of miles had rolled beneath the tires before Dan got to the point where he had graduated from high school and was looking into a career. He'd at first intended on going to an automotive technical institute to become professionally trained to service cars. He'd also considered going into the armed forces.

"But then I was approached by someone who made me an interesting offer. There are rookie drivers, and I was offered a position as a rookie mechanic. It seemed a dream come true. At first my folks were against it, but when money talks, a lot of people listen, and they realized that I could have a very good life ahead of me. So I went to work for this racing family. I did the mechanical work.

"As a mechanic," Dan seemed to rush on, "there are times when you feel you can only really diagnose something by seeing how the machine handles. Or hearing it from behind the wheel. So it was natural for me to take the racers out on the track—"

"And you fell in love with speed," A.J. murmured.

"That's about it. Then the people I worked for, who'd been watching me, concluded that not only was I a pretty good mechanic, but I was also a steady driver with excellent reflexes and instincts. I was grateful that they gave me a shot at driving their cars, considering that I wasn't one of them."

"So what made you give it up?" A.J. asked. "I

know you never totaled a racer out or hit the wall because you said that you started to begin imagining that—"

"What caused it was a big race," Dan said, not bothering to name it. "A guy was killed. I wasn't racing. I was in the pit crew. But any time that happens—well, what with your brother getting killed at the race—you know exactly what I'm talking about. It really gets through to everyone. It makes you stop and think. At least it made me start to stop and think."

"Yes, Kip's death bothered Dad. And me. And others."

"My mother had been worried constantly about my career as a race driver. My folks lived a long ways away. I called home whenever I got the chance, and my mother wrote to me regularly. She'd begun going to a church. When she got actively involved, Dad joined in, too. About that time, Mom started enclosing little tracts with her letters. They started to make me think."

"I know what that's like. Beth keeps some in her purse so they're handy if she feels a need to present one to somebody."

"At first I discounted her Christian philosophies based on biblical teachings. You know how young adults can be. They think that their parents are unsophisticated and don't know what it's like out there in the big, wide world." Dan gave a rueful laugh. "But my small-town, homemaking mother was a plenty smart woman. At least she started me thinking about the purpose of my life."

"And—"

"And I found myself thinking about it—and about God—even when I didn't want to. I'd wake up in the night, feeling like I wasn't quite living right, even though I wasn't actually living all that wrong."

"That must have been uncomfortable."

"Not really uncomfortable so much as feeling that something was faintly out of tune—like my life needed correcting. An adjustment, so to speak. Or a tuneup. I began to think about dying. It was a frightening thought. So I tried to outrun it by racing even faster. I thought that if I could hit high enough speeds, my upsetting thoughts couldn't catch up with me."

"And of course you failed."

"Sure did," Dan said. He glanced at A.J. "You sound like you know what that's like."

"I do."

"It's my hope that you'll find out what my other experiences were like, too," he said. "Anyway, when that driver was killed in an unfortunate accident that shouldn't have happened, we were all devastated. There were a lot of people laying blame, and there were others saying it couldn't have been avoided. Everyone seemed to have a point of view about whether the accident was avoidable or unavoidable.

"I listened to them, and eventually I considered one of the tracts that my mother had sent me. About how we are born to die, and that there's a time for everything. I knew that, sad as it was and as traumatic as the event turned out to be, it'd been that driver's moment to return to the Creator. His death became the catalyst to bring others to the Lord."

"The accident had happened so fast," Dan continued. "I know it was jarring to everyone to realize that one moment the driver was with us, and the next moment he was gone into eternity. I started thinking of things Mama had said. I found myself hoping that the driver was right with the Lord. That he'd been ready to go to God."

Dan fell silent.

"And?" A.J. prompted. Her voice was tight, strangled by the dry lump that indicated welling tears deep within.

Dan gripped the steering wheel hard. "That's when I realized that I wasn't ready to face God. And that I was risking not only my earthly life but my eternal life racing around the track aiming for increased speed and faster time trials."

"So you gave it up?"

"Oh, not right away," Dan said. "You know what human nature's like. I hoped it'd go away, that my old, peaceful, unconcerned outlook would come back."

Dan told A.J. how he had tried to at least ignore the nagging thoughts if he couldn't put them from his mind. "But the Lord doesn't give up on us just because we may give up on Him," Dan said. "Others thought that I was losing my nerve behind the wheel. But what I was being relieved of was my obsession with speed. I no longer craved it."

"Ah, so then you gave it up?"

"Yes. And no. I gave up driving to become a full-time mechanic again. That way I could stay in the racing business to serve others."

"If it was so wrong for you to race, Dan, how could it be right for you to be a mechanic?"

"Some missionaries go to Africa or other Third World countries. I considered that racetracks and race drivers and pit crews would be my special ministry. When someone was hurting or in spiritual need, I wanted to be there. And when someone was obsessed with speed as I once was and was willing to risk it all to win a race, I wanted to be there.

"I wanted to maintain that racer at its peak so that the driver could count on performance and faultless mechanical work. In that way I could do my part to keep someone alive. What I've been doing is buying time for dare-devils in hopes that by doing so, they'll live long enough to be moved to seek the Lord as their personal Savior."

"So that's your story," A.J. breathed.

"Yes. Some men preach from a pulpit."

"And you practice what is preached in the pit."

"Yes."

A.J. was silent a long moment. "I'm really glad to have you as part of my team, Dan."

"Thanks. But the team you need to become a part of is God's. The Rick Stacy family is legendary. But the family of God is more important. A relationship that doesn't end with earthly life but continues into eternity."

"I'll think about it," A.J. said, as she found him telling her things Beth—and Jill—had recently said. They all used different words, but those words carried an identical meaning.

"That's all I'd ask. That's all the Lord would ask. He wants you, A.J. But you have a free will, and the Lord respects that. You must humble yourself, recognize your need, and open your heart to invite Him to fully enter your life. Then you can live, forever hidden in Him."

ten

A.J.'s pulse grew to a triphammer beat when Dan pulled the Stacy transport into an assigned slot and shut off the engine.

For a moment she sat without motion, feeling almost overwhelmed to be a part of a big racing event again. Everywhere she looked she saw a familiar face. She knew it was an experience shared by Dan.

No sooner had the pair exited the transport than they were greeted by old friends and hailed by other acquaintances who quickly became lost in the milling crowd. Within a minute, Dan and A.J. were parted by a crush of people.

A.J. was touched by her warm welcome at the track. She felt as if she were bathed in a golden glow of well-being. But just as suddenly she grew ice cold. A shard of suspicion pierced her thoughts, seeming to impale her with accelerating distrust.

A.J. stared, feeling as if she couldn't manage to breathe. Even as her mind tried to present logical explanations, her heart responded with irrational, infuriated emotions when she witnessed Dan Barenfanger greet Duke Carrington. The two men laughed, exchanged bear hugs, and thumped each other on the biceps as they exuberantly expressed their joy in seeing each other at the trackside reunion.

A.J. was glazed into rigid inaction. She couldn't stop staring, even though she felt vulnerable, knowing the look that was on her face. She hoped no one would notice.

With great effort, A.J. tore herself from the scene only a heartbeat before she knew Dan would have turned in her direction and intercepted her incredulous stare. On quaking legs, A.J. made her way to their assigned area and waited for Dan to arrive with the transport.

En route, she met old friends and stopped to exchange brief pleasantries, managing to force a light-hearted gaiety to her tone. Inside, however, she was numb.

A minute later, Dan unloaded the racer and the whirlwind of activity lessened. A.J. took a moment to collect herself, then briskly set about her prerace duties. By the time she was involved in her assigned chores, she had begun to recover emotionally. It was no longer so patently evident that she was in turmoil. But deep inside she was still suffering churning sensations that threatened to suck her down into an eddying whirlpool of bad memories and unpleasant feelings.

"How's it going, A.J.?" Dan asked in an easy tone as he joined her.

She flashed him a bright, confident smile.

"Just fine," she replied, hoping that he couldn't detect the chaotic thoughts and emotions that warred within her. And she hoped that Dan—hardworking, loyal Dan—would never suspect that she longed to rage at him. If only to relieve her tensions, she would love to demand from him an explanation of just what Duke Carrington had meant to him in the past.

A.J.'s mind swirled with possible preambles to lead into such a touchy topic, but they were interrupted by a knock.

"Anyone here? Danny Boy, you in there?" a voice called out.

"Yeah!" Dan replied, setting aside a tool, squinting toward the slash of bright light from the outside.

An elderly man limped in.

"I'll be," Dan said. "Sonny Jackson, how good to see you! I knew I'd run across a lot of the guys, but I never dreamed we'd meet face to face."

"I go to what races retirement checks allow me to attend."

Quickly Dan made introductions, including A.J., who went about her work. She afforded the older man only a small smile when he laid a gnarled hand on the racer's body, stroking it as if it were a living being. Mr. Jackson shook his head.

"I remember when your daddy used to drive this car, girl," he said in a soft tone. "I hope you're big enough to handle the steering wheel a man like Rick Stacy left vacant."

"She is," Dan assured. "We're going to show the world. A.J.'s going to be Indy bound before the dust settles."

"Well the best of luck to you, miss!" Sonny Jackson said before he turned back to Dan. "I was hoping maybe we'd get a chance to share some chitchat about the old days, Dan. Need any help? It'd feel good to be of use to someone again."

"No. Thanks anyway. A.J. and I have it under control," Dan dismissed. "But I'd like to see you, too." He glanced at his watch. "I reckon we could get together and grab a quick cup of coffee."

"You're on, boy. Green flags all the way. What time?"

"Thirty minutes okay for you?"

"Super. I'll check back then."

"I should be ready. A.J.'ll stay with the car till race-time."

"I won't keep you long."

The man ran his fingertips the length of the sleek racer, seemed to shake his head over the nostalgic memories, then limped from the area.

"You have a lot of friends in the racing industry," A.J. said. "More than I do." She was about to mention Duke Carrington, but Dan replied before she could raise her old enemy's name.

"Yeah, I've been blessed," he said. And he made the utterance with such a finality that A.J. knew the topic of Dan Barenfanger's friends was closed to any further discussion until they'd completed their normal preparatory routines.

Or was he blocking her out on purpose? Not giving her the chance to raise questions about a man he'd perhaps had dealings with? There were times when Dan had seemed to have almost uncanny insights into her. It was as if he could penetrate her defenses and see right into her mind, plumbing the depths of her very soul.

Was he aware that she was upset by his relationship with Duke Carrington—and who knew who else—and was he doing what he could to postpone or prevent a confrontation that delineated loyalties?

Steeped in her nettlesome, confidence-shaking thoughts, A.J. didn't notice the time pass. Abruptly, she was aware that Dan had stopped whistling, a sure sign that he was done.

"Right on time!" he announced as he finished.

Almost as if on cue, Sonny Jackson returned.

"Ready to go, Danny Boy?"

"With bells on," the younger man replied.

"You'll stay with the car, won't you, A.J.?" Dan asked.

She nodded. "I'll be right here."

"Good girl," Dan said. "We won't be long. I'll be back in plenty of time."

A.J. stared after the pair as they left, then she jerked her thoughts back to her own list of prerace tasks. She sighed and kicked the tire of Rick Stacy's racer in disgusted consternation when she realized that her concentration was so poor that she'd just begun to repeat a task she'd already performed. She'd been so absorbed in her thoughts from the past that, while she'd gone through the motions of her prerace check, she had no idea what the results had been.

She'd have to do better—would do better—once she was out on the long oval track.

eleven

The din on the race track was almost deafening, but even so A.J. was aware of her heart thundering with excitement as she moved into her place in the starting lineup. She strained through her goggles for the signal that the race was on.

Those first moments of the race could be among the most important, A.J. knew, for so often whoever managed to jockey into the lead stayed there. Being caught behind was where talent and the condition of the racer became vitally important. Precious seconds shaved off could close the car lengths between those who would see prize money and those who would return home empty handed.

Adrenaline hit A.J.'s system with a helpful spurt when the race began. The first few minutes she was edgy. Only when she made the moves that put her into second place in the lineup of whining racers did she exhale and realize that she'd been driving with bated breath.

Her heart sang when she realized that only Ronnie Smith was ahead of her. Duke Carrington had gotten off to a poor start and was trapped far, far behind in a melange of cars.

A.J. was into her twelfth lap of the one hundred mile race when she moved into position to begin her ploy to overtake Ronnie Smith and capture the lead. With luck she could then retain it all the way to the finish line and walk away from the track the speedway's big winner for the day.

Ronnie wasn't going to give up the lead without a fight, she realized. He did all that he could to prevent A.J. from using anything to her advantage, be it the tail wind as they both shot down the straightaway with the breeze at their backs or the laws of physics.

Physics was something that all drivers understood to various degrees. There was veteran ace driver Tony Bettenhausen who so wanted to spread the knowledge of physics that he used his Gasoline Alley garage at the Indy 500 race track to film an educational video. It was developed by three professors from Ball State University and illustrated principles of friction, the Doppler effect, and the changes in sound waves—all of which are demonstrated and used on the race track every day. While they might not comprehend the theories involved, all drivers understood in a very practical way how the laws of physics worked.

A.J. and Ronnie, dueling racers, were winding up the fifteenth lap, and A.J. was slowly gaining. Inch by precious inch she began to draw even with him.

Ronnie's jawline was determined, she noticed, when she glanced across and saw his rigid profile. Although she was beginning to leave him behind, she knew that he was no more grimly determined than she to win the race.

A.J. sighed with relief when she maneuvered her father's racer solidly into the lead position. Fans would go wild over a neck and neck race, she knew, but A.J. was intent on denying them such an afternoon's thrill. She wanted to put as many car lengths as possible between herself and the number two racer.

As she inched ahead, Ronnie maintained a steady position. She had to tear a full car length from him by what seemed a centimeter at a time.

Soon there was one length.

Then two.

Finally, there were three lengths separating them!

A.J. sighed and managed to shrug against her restraint system. Even with such a solid lead, it was difficult to relax.

A glance in her rearview mirror assured her that she had Ronnie Smith under control. It was Duke Carrington who was coming up fast. Duke may have gotten off to a sluggish start, impeded by lesser drivers who blocked his way, but his years of experience had stood him in good stead. He'd made the right maneuvers and was obviously making up for lost time.

A.J.'s heart gave a nervous gallop when she understood that her enemy in the personal realm was her prime contender in her professional world as well.

A.J. was beginning her seventeenth lap. By then Ronnie had lost the number two slot to

Duke, who was still coming on strong.

He'd closed the gap at an alarming rate by the time they zoomed into lap number eighteen.

Tension was such that by lap number twenty, A.J. was bathed in perspiration. She didn't know how she could endure the stress of knowing that Duke's goggled face was reflected in her rearview mirror, looking so close it was as if she could touch him.

Anger stormed through A.J. as she considered the possibility that Duke was toying with her. He might be hoping to psyche her out by using stress as a racing tool in the same way as he would manipulate his car, given the opportunity.

A.J. glanced back and saw a subtle sideways drift in Duke's car that filled the entire frame of her rearview mirror. She knew that the moment had come when he was going to make his move.

Count on him to do it in a grandstanding manner, she thought bitterly. They were rounding the curve, their engines screaming. Then both cars thundered down the straightaway where to the right, the grandstand and bleacher sections were jammed with cheering racing enthusiasts.

At the instant Duke swung out to make his bid to call out more horses from his powerful engine, thereby exceeding the momentary capabilities of A.J.'s racer, the dummy lights slightly above eye level in her car lit up like the Fourth of July.

A.J. wasn't sure, but she believed that she'd felt a momentary loss of power—like a hiccup— before the powerful engine caught and resumed as strong as ever. She stared at the idiot lights, wondering if it was only a false alarm or a circuitry problem, rather than something more serious.

But her desperate hopes were dashed when a thin plume of smoke fanned up to assault her nostrils. For a moment she hoped that it was merely the stench from Duke's exhaust system. Then with a gasp of horror, she saw a wispy tongue of flame lick up to be blown back at her. The wiring—something—was on fire.

A.J. was so rattled that when the power system began to fail, she wrenched the wheel hard, battling it before it was fully necessary. She almost propelled her car into Duke's racer in her haste to get as close as possible to the fire-fighting apparatus and trained personnel standing by.

Shocked, dazed, humiliated, she realized that she'd unthinkingly cut Duke off—dangerously so. His driving expertise had saved them, but by mere centimeters.

Duke moved into the lead position as A.J. fell away. She drove toward the sidelines like a wounded bird, crippling away from the flock of racers speeding by.

Tears were streaming down A.J.'s cheeks when she unbuckled her restraint system. She ran clear of the car and watched the soft foam splat as it quelled the flames and saved her father's racer from more extensive damage.

Suddenly, Dan was there.

Gratefully she collapsed into his arms, weeping.

"Shhhh," he said as he held her. "It's okay. We'll fix it good as new. I've seen a lot worse. Worked on worse."

"That's one relief," A.J. sighed.

The legacy lived on. Her father's car would race again.

twelve

A.J. stood off to the side, clutching the metal and flame-blackened plastic screwdriver that had caused all the commotion. Her ravaged face watched the incapacitated racer get loaded onto the transport, positioned, then secured.

Drivers milled around offering Dan and A.J. their condolences along with assurances that A.J.'s car would soon be good as new.

"Ready to roll, A.J.?" Dan asked when he'd double-checked the load for stability.

"Yes," she murmured in a weak voice.

A.J. kept her eyes on the ground, not encouraging anyone to address her. That had been her reaction the entire time as people had wandered by to view the racer.

She had waited for someone to make a remark about the fact that she'd cut off Duke Carrington, dangerously so, in what could have been a devastating accident resulting in a major pileup of cars.

No one had said a word, and she felt worse—even more guilty—in the face of their silence. She'd have almost felt relief if someone had railed at her. Then she could have defended herself, offered excuses, pointed out extenuating circumstances.

But no one made a move to accuse A.J. Stacy except for her own festering conscience.

A part of her wanted to approach Duke Carrington

and tell him that she was sorry—as he'd apologized to her and her father years before. But pride and uncertainty stopped her from taking such action. He might ignore her. Or worse, he could fling her apology back in her face.

Sighing, A.J. decided that it was better to say nothing than to risk causing the situation to grow worse.

She was preparing to climb into the cab of the transport when Sonny Jackson came toward them, walking as fast as his limp would allow. He seemed to be somewhat riled, but he was trying desperately not to let it show.

"What're the chances of me bumming a ride with you all?" He got right to the point. "If you don't mind, I'd like to go as far as you can take me, then catch a bus for home."

Dan shot A.J. a questioning look, his eyes offering an appeal on the old man's behalf. She realized that they could spare the elderly man the need to part with precious funds.

"You're welcome to ride along," she said in a gracious tone.

Sonny Jackson seemed to wilt with relief.

"Sure was tough luck you had, miss. But you have to accept the bad same's you do the good," he offered philosophically.

"Mmmm," A. J. murmured and settled back for the long ride.

Dan eased the transport into gear and rolled into line behind some of the other teams heading for various destinations.

"I couldn't believe what happened to the racer," Dan said, and shook his head with incredulity.

"It's a freak situation," Sonny said. "But over the years when I worked in pit crews, I saw some jim-dandy oddball accidents take place. I've seen this exact incident. Sometimes it ended with no damage and a mechanic making the discovery. Or else it landed up with a racer worse off than Rick Stacy's car."

"But A.J. and I are so careful," Dan mused, "that I can't fathom how it came to turn out like this."

"Accidents happen," Sonny said in a matter-of-fact tone that seemed to suggest he wasn't interested in plumbing assorted possibilities.

"You don't suppose someone sabotaged us, do you?" Dan queried, frowning.

"Anything's possible," Sonny said. "But I thought Rick's girl was going to stay with the car when we went for coffee."

"I did," A.J. quietly stressed. "No one came near it."

"Then no one had the chance," Dan said. "The only ones around it after I unloaded it from the transport were A.J., you, and me."

"Well, I never even touch—" Sonny started to say.

But with a glance in A.J.'s direction, he seemed to realize that she clearly recalled that he had touched the racer.

Twice.

Sonny changed the subject, and Dan followed his lead. The two men fell into easy conversation as the wheels rolled off the miles. The hum of the tires against hot pavement and the men's droning conversation helped A.J. to begin to relax as she tried to think back through the hours preceding the racing events.

She and Dan had done their assigned tasks, adhering to the routine they'd perfected back at Stacy Speedway.

Their scheduled sharing of the preparatory tasks prevented wasted time spent in unwitting duplications. It also helped them to avoid accidentally overlooking an important detail because they assumed the other had attended to that matter.

A.J. recalled how flustered she had felt earlier that day. She remembered how piqued she'd felt to realize she'd performed the same task twice with almost no memory of the earlier action. Could she as easily have overlooked another detail? Could she have had her thoughts drawn from the matter at hand and left the now-mangled screwdriver lying near the engine block?

The tool had probably ridden in the car on a mechanical ledge created by the housing. The swaying during the race had caused it to jostle and roll. Eventually, it had fallen into the bowels of the powerhouse and rested against the hot motor until its plastic handle had melted. The resulting liquid had run down the motor, reached the kindling point, and burst into flames. Inevitably, this had set the racer's wiring on fire.

On the other hand, was she being too willing to blame herself because she knew she had been in error when she cut Duke Carrington off on the raceway?

Could it be that Sonny Jackson, who seemed like a harmless old man devoted to the racing world, was actually an enemy in disguise? He certainly could pass through the various pit crews undetected and unsuspected.

Was the fact that he'd begged a ride of them a mere coincidence? Or was he trying to allay any suspicions they might have? Ordinarily, the guilty party wouldn't dream of being with them in the hours immediately following such devastation.

A.J. didn't know. But she was certain that they would have to be wary of those allowed near the racer—and more careful than ever about their own performances.

thirteen

When Dan downshifted the transport rig, A.J. was jolted awake. Then the men's soft voices penetrated her mind. She sat up and realized that she'd drifted off to sleep somewhere between the race track and home. She was unsure how long she'd slept, but she knew that it had been quite a while. She felt rested.

"We're almost home, sleepyhead," Dan teased.

"Felt good," A.J. yawned.

Dan faced Sonny. "You may as well stick with us," he said. "I'll haul this rig to the speedway. A.J. can head for her apartment, and after I've stowed everything and given the premises a once-over, then we can go to my place. You may as well bunk at my apartment. We can worry about getting you to the bus station for a ticket out tomorrow. How's that sound?"

"Sounds fine with me, boy," Sonny agreed. "I've been enjoying all this reminiscing about the old days."

"Good enough," Dan said. "Then that's what we'll do."

He left the interstate, proceeded through the city, then headed onto a highway that led to the outskirts and Stacy Speedway.

The area was deserted except for the few cars in the parking lot. Security lights illuminated the area, but the glow that startled both A.J. and Dan was the light shining from the windows of the office building.

"Why, Beth's car is still in the parking lot!" A.J. said. "And it's way past quitting time."

"I wonder what she's doing here?" Dan said, and his voice sounded as puzzled as A.J. felt.

"We'll find out soon enough," she said.

No sooner had Dan rolled to a halt than Beth came bustling from the office building. Ordinarily she wore a jovial, congenial expression. But that night her brow was furrowed with concern, and she wore an aura of disaster.

"I'm so glad you're back," she began in a rush before anyone in the trio climbing from the transport could speak. "Dan, I'm afraid that we received some bad news about two hours ago. I considered calling the State Police to have them intercept you with a message, but I decided to allow a little more time for you to show up."

"Oh, no," he whispered. "What?"

"It's your mother, Dan. They called this afternoon. She had a heart attack—"

"Is she—?"

"She's in the hospital, in the coronary care unit. The doctors have administered that drug—I forget the name of it—but it can prevent damage to the heart muscle if—"

"Praise the Lord," Dan whispered, visibly relieved.

"Your mother is still in crisis, Dan, but the doctors say that she's doing as well as can be expected. She's not out of danger yet, and your father asked me to tell you that everyone is doing what's humanly possible. It's in the Lord's hands. I've been praying," Beth added, "and I've already got my prayer partners involved, too."

"Thanks, Beth. That means so much to me."

"I also asked Jill to pray for your mother's full recovery, when she checked in to see if A.J. had returned."

"This changes things," Dan mused. He fell silent as if caught on the horns of dilemma. A.J. realized that he wanted—needed—to be with his mother and father. But he also knew that they relied on him at Stacy Speedway.

"You'll be leaving tonight, Dan, won't you?" A.J. said smoothly. "Tell me—us—what to do so we can help you get ready to roll. You must go to your mother's side."

Dan gave her a grateful look as she purposely made his decision easier for him. "At the moment I can hardly think, let alone draw up an intelligent list of specifics."

"Well," Beth prefaced. Then, in a crisp, no-nonsense, unrattled voice she began issuing orders to those grouped around her, Sonny included, instructing them on what to do.

Twenty minutes later, Dan unlocked his car, ready to leave. "Thanks for helping out like this. I really appreciate it."

"You'd have done the same and more for any one of us," Beth said. "You just go on now, and don't worry your head for a moment about us.

You've got quite enough to think about."

"I do worry, though. I hate having to take off like this and leave you in the lurch. I'll try to get back just as soon as I can. Maybe I can fly down here for the stock car competition dates and then rush back to the hospital if my family still needs me."

"Beth's right, Dan," A.J. stressed. "Don't worry about it. We'll get by. Be with your family. That's what's important now. I'm very sorry you're facing this trouble. I know what it's like. I hope that your mother will be just fine, and that your father and your family will be able to cope."

"I know that everyone's prayers for our family will bring us the strength we need to face whatever is ahead," Dan replied. "God brings us such comfort in times like these."

For a moment A.J. was shaken. Dan talked as if prayer was something as familiar as talking to a beloved friend. As if it was communication that was as direct as when she talked to Jill or Beth. He was as confident that God would hear his prayers as she had been that her parents would take her seriously when she asked them for something that was terribly important to her.

For a moment, A.J. felt as if she were going to cry. She longed to be part of a group that trusted in God for everything. She was so tired of being alone.

As if sensing her loneliness, Dan gave A.J. a hug and brushed his lips quickly across her cheek. Then he moved on to accept Beth's motherly embrace and consoling words.

"I'll be going by my apartment, Sonny," Dan said. "You're welcome to bunk there. I can give you directions to the bus term—Hey!" Dan gasped "Maybe Sonny's our answer—"

"What?" the elderly man said, perplexed.

"Do you have to return home right away?" Dan abruptly questioned.

"Well, no," the retiree said, his manner a bit hesitant. "I used to have to be around to pick up my social security check. But now I have them send it right to the bank."

"Would you consider remaining here and filling in for me while I have to be away?" Dan asked. "I'd give you the key to my apartment, and I know A.J. could find something for you to drive back and forth. We'd pay you for your time, and—"

"Gee, I don't know," Sonny said. "I hang around racetracks as much as I can, but it's been a while since I've worked. I might not be—"

"Bosh! You'd be just wonderful," Beth interrupted by reassuring the older man. "Dan's got everything in such order that there'd be nothing to it. If you had a question, A.J. or I could provide the answer."

"And if they couldn't, I'd be only a phone call away," Dan pointed out.

"Please, Sonny? We need you," A.J. said, knowing that Sonny seemed to have detected her reservations about him. "You knew my father. You could consider it a favor to the late Rick Stacy and Dan Barenfanger, if nothing else. Although I'd be very grateful."

"I'd be honored, miss, to be associated, even briefly, with Stacy Speedway," Sonny declared.

"Then you're hired," A.J. said softly. "See you tomorrow!"

Beth and A.J. stood outside the office building and watched until the red lights on the rear of Dan's Thunderbird disappeared into the night.

"Well, I guess we can go home now," Beth said. "I'm ready to call it a day."

"A very long day," A.J. said, and told her about the race. "Any messages for me other than Jill's call?"

"Uh-uh," Beth said. "Once the parking lot cleared out after the race yesterday, everything just went to sleep so I got caught up around the office. Nothing happened that I couldn't handle."

"Great. I don't know what I'd do without you, Beth. I'll never be able to let you retire!" A.J. glanced at her wristwatch. "It's not too late, so I guess I'll give Jill a call. She'll want to know the latest update you received about Dan's mother, and I'm sure she'll be interested in how we're going to handle business in Dan's absence."

"I have a good feeling about Sonny," Beth admitted. "This could be a blessing in disguise. Maybe even our answer."

"What do you mean?" A.J. asked. She could see nothing in the terrible events to find joy in, much less an answer to any of the myriad of problems she faced.

"You and Dan have been talking about how you

need someone to help out here while you're away racing. You've hesitated over hiring a manager."

Suddenly A.J. caught the drift.

"Beth, you're right! Our solution could be found in Sonny Jackson!"

A moment later, goose bumps rippled over her skin when she recalled the bantering conversation with Dan. She'd wanted to hire a manager. Dan had begged for one more week. A.J. had said that perhaps they could find someone for a part-time position. Dan had jokingly countered that perhaps they might hope for free-lance involvement, which they both knew would require a minor miracle.

Suddenly, A.J. realized that with Sonny Jackson, they indeed might have the answer to some pressing speedway problems.

"We'll see how he works out," A.J. promised. "And I'll talk it over with Dan. If everything goes as you're praying it will, when Dan returns he can make Sonny an offer. Let's hope it will be something Sonny can't refuse."

fourteen

A.J. was out of breath when the hostess at Granny's Kitchen showed her to the table where Jill Alexander was seated.

"Hi! Sorry I'm late."

"Something come up at the office?"

"You've got that right," A.J. muttered. "There's always something. Even with Sonny Jackson helping out, what with Dan gone, I almost meet myself coming and going. Some days I really wonder if it's worth it."

"Lower your voice," Jill said, "or that remark might get back to Duke Carrington and give him fresh hope that you're considering selling out."

A.J. gave a light laugh. "A few more days like today, and I'd be desperate enough to call him."

"I wasn't exactly joking," Jill said, and leaned forward, purportedly to better scan the menu that the waitress had set before her. "Don't look now, but that's our sportswriter seated across the room with the pretty brunette."

"Oh!" A.J. gave a startled gasp, then clamped her lips shut as she perused the menu.

"Have you heard any more from Dan?" Jill asked.

"We spoke this morning. His mother's doing better."

"Praise the Lord. Any word on when he hopes to

be back on the job?" Jill inquired.

"By the end of the week," A.J. said. "Although that's tentative, you understand."

"Bet you'll be ready to throw a 'Welcome Home, Dan!' party, eh?" Jill teased.

"You'd better believe it. I really miss that man."

"In a personal or a professional capacity?" Jill asked, her eyes twinkling.

A.J. smoothed her hair away from her cheeks that suddenly seemed warm and flushed.

"Is this off the record?"

"Of course."

"Both."

"I thought so," Jill said, pleased. "I talked to Dan myself," she admitted. "I posed the same question to him."

"And?"

"Got the identical answer."

A.J.'s heart skipped a beat. Her fingers trembled as she lifted the menu and appeared to study it with unconcern. She felt giddy with hope at the news that Dan was as attracted to her as she was to him.

"It's been a tough week," A.J. said when she felt like she could control her voice. "Dan's really been through a lot. He's close to his mother, you know, so it's been very wrenching. It would have been awful if she'd died."

"Yes, but at least he'd have had the comfort of knowing that he'd been a good son," Jill mused. "A devoted son."

A.J. stiffened. Her voice caught. "And just

what's that supposed to mean?" she inquired in a cool, tight tone.

Jill looked up in surprise. "Nothing, dear. I was simply stating a fact." She frowned. "Oh. I see. You thought that I was offering an opinion?"

A.J. nodded. "It crossed my mind."

Jill laughed. "You should know that my modus operandi is to be more direct than that. But if my casual remark caused you a twinge of discomfort, then maybe the topic does bear being explored."

A.J. had found herself thinking about her mother more than she liked that week. Thinking was bad enough. Talking might be more than she could handle.

"Please, Jill, I'd rather not."

"There are a lot of things in life you'd rather not. If you didn't have a career as a race driver, my friend, you'd be a natural to go out for women's track. You're an expert at running away. You're a big girl, A.J., so maybe it's time that I told you a few things—whether you want to hear them or not."

"Because you're such a good friend?" A.J. asked a bit sarcastically.

Jill shrugged. "Yup! What are friends for?"

"I'm beginning to wonder," A.J. grumped, sighing as she realized that Jill was going to have her say.

The reporter accepted her soft drink from the waitress, then moved it closer, smoothing the circle of moisture on the checked table cloth with her manicured index fingertip.

"You know, I was thinking, as you probably have been, that it so easily could have been you that got bad news while you were away at the race, instead of Dan."

"I . . . I'm aware of that."

"Your mother is not a young woman anymore, A.J., and while she's in reasonably good health, she has her problems, too, as do most people in their so-called golden years. Physically, Liz Stacy is coping very nicely. Trim, fit, and Florida-tan. But emotionally? Well, I don't like to be the bearer of bad news, but your mom's not doing so well. Your differences are taking a toll on her."

"How do you know?" A.J. asked. "You've been in touch with her?"

Jill nodded. "Occasionally."

A.J. felt unreasonable anger surge through her. "What right have you to meddle in my life? And my mother's?"

"I'd hardly call it meddling, A.J., and if nothing else, it's my professional duty. You mother subscribes to the paper, and every so often I receive a letter from her regarding the personal interest features bearing my byline. And," Jill said, offering a wry smile, "I always answer my fan mail."

"I see."

A.J. tried to keep a disinterested demeanor, but it wasn't easy. At the moment, it was a matter of pride. She didn't want Jill to rush back to her apartment and call or write Liz Stacy to share the juicy tidbit that A.J. indeed did miss her mommy. Not even if the bald truth was that she had—

terribly—and for so very long. That ache of absence had been made even worse with Dan gone. During the past week, she had come to the growing realization that one day a call could come for her, announcing that her mother had met an untimely death.

A.J. considered the unanswered letters from her mother. The unreturned phone calls on her answering machine. She squirmed with discomfort when she realized how unapproachable she'd been. How unforgiving. How unrepentant for her own errors in attitude.

She felt her face grow crimson when she realized that Jill Alexander knew that it was more A.J.'s fault than her mother's that the estrangement continued.

A.J. sought a carefree, uninvolved tack.

"I'm glad Mother has you, Jill, considering that you and I were such close girlhood friends. I'm sure she finds you a great comfort."

"As a matter of fact, she does," Jill admitted, nonplussed and dead set on needling. "In many ways I've become the daughter to her that you've chosen not to be. She needs someone, A.J. Until you decide to shape up and stop acting like a spoiled brat, I'm it."

A.J.'s eyes narrowed. "Why, you!"

Further furious words were held at bay as the waitress approached. "Ready to order now?"

A.J. felt like storming out, but she was hungry and knew deep down that Jill was right. Furthermore, she didn't want to create a scene when

Granny's Kitchen was filled with diners, including the sportswriter for the *Daily News*. She had caught him scrutinizing her and Jill several times.

Forcing a serene tone and a pleasant smile, she managed to present her order.

No sooner had the waitress departed with their orders than the sportswriter and his date left their table and made their way toward the cashier.

"Hi, Maggie. Tom," Jill greeted the pair. "Have a nice meal?"

"Tops," Tom said, patting his stomach. Maggie grinned, nodding, as she murmured agreement.

"Have you met A.J. Stacy?" Jill asked.

"I don't believe I've had the pleasure," Tom replied. "I've been at the speedway, but our paths haven't crossed."

"Then I'll make introductions so it's official," Jill said. She did the honors, being careful to include Tom's girlfriend.

"I've been hearing good things about Stacy Speedway lately," Tom said. "I've been told you have a new man around—Dan Barenfanger."

"That's right," A.J. said.

She winced, sitting up straight in her chair, when she received a sharp tap from the point of Jill's shoe. Her friend, A.J. realized, was giving her a quick reminder to be on guard around the reporter who covered the sporting world.

"Would that be *the* Dan Barenfanger?" Tom asked.

"Well, I'm assuming so," A.J. said, "To us he is *the* Dan Barenfanger, and Beth Carter is *the* Beth

Carter, and Jill Alexander is *the* Jill Alexander, and Sonny Jackson is *the* Sonny Jackson—"

"Are you kidding me?" Tom asked. "You've got Sonny Jackson on your payroll?"

"Well, yes, temporarily. He's helping out," she replied. "He knew my father many years ago."

"That would have to have been when Rick Stacy was first starting out, right?"

"I'm sure it was," A.J. said. "I never met the racetrack greats from those years. I'm not the best with names," she admitted.

"Cars, it's another thing," Jill broke in, laughingly supporting A.J.'s weakness. "If it's a vehicle, she can see it once and almost tell you its registration number."

"I'm not that bad," A.J. defended.

"Well, you're not very good, either. Not like Tom here," Jill said. "Whip a name at that boy and he can read you the individual's pedigree and his or her entire past."

"Oh, were but that I was as good as Jill says," Tom murmured, winking at A.J. "I always do my homework. I use my modem and tap into what's able to be accumulated via computer networks. Of course, I happen to be blessed with a retentive mind."

"He has a memory like an elephant," Maggie chimed in.

"Great work aids on the job, I'm sure," A.J. remarked.

"It sounds like you've got a super support staff at Stacy Speedway. Have you got any special plans you can talk about?"

"Only that I hope to be Indy bound," A.J. said.

Tom nodded. "That goes without saying. As does the fact that you'll want Dan Barenfanger on your team. You've got such a great team amassed, A.J., I'd really like to do some interviews. You. Dan. Sonny. Maybe even Beth, who could represent the little person behind the big names we read about. What do you say?"

"Sounds good."

"I do pieces for the *Daily News,* but I also work as a stringer for some of the sports magazines on a freelance basis, so there'd be various levels of exposure. All of it could be helpful as you're Indy bound."

"How wonderful."

"Now that we're about to roll into winter and you'll be closing Stacy Speedway for stock car competition while you concentrate on the upcoming races, perhaps you and your staff could spare me some time to conduct the interviews?"

"I'm sure we could," A.J. agreed.

"We can shoot some film, too, and I can write the articles, then check back with you when racing season is going full tilt so that I can include any last minute updates. What do you say?"

"I say—terrific!"

Tom extracted a business card and slid it across the table to her.

"Nice meeting you, A.J. Good seeing you, Jill," he said and cheerfully tapped his coworker on the shoulder. "See you at the office. I'll be in touch, A.J."

"Terrific. We'll be looking forward to it, Tom, and my staff will have orders to give you their complete cooperation."

"Until then," he said, giving the pair a brief wave as he and Maggie made their way to the cashier's station.

"Well, that was a surprise," A.J. said. "We can use all of the good publicity we can get. Locally and nationwide."

"I hope that's all that comes of it."

"What do you mean now, Eeyore?" A.J. asked.

"Tom Findlay is one of the most thorough reporters I've ever met. He leaves no stone unturned. So, if you've got a few rocks you'd rather not have disturbed, hope that they're buried under too many layers of distracting strata for Tom to ever unearth them."

"That bad?"

"Uh-huh," Jill assented. "If it's happened to you, Tom Findlay will probably find out about it. And if you desperately wish to keep the tidbit private, Tom Findlay will consider it his patriotic, civic-minded, gossip-fueling duty to publicly tell the world. That guy can dig up dirt that people didn't even know they had a need to hide."

"Jill, no! Tell me that you're teasing."

"If only I could, A.J.," Jill moaned. "If only I could."

"But what am I going to do?" A.J. whispered. She could feel her stomach tie up in such a tight knot that her appetite disappeared without a trace.

"If I were in your shoes, honey, the first thing

I'd do is go home and call my mother and make peace with her so there's nothing there for Tom to write about. And then I'd call in my employees and set them in the corner of a dreary room with a 1000-watt light bulb shining in their eyes. I would hold them prisoner until they admitted to any little transgression on down to and including jaywalking while en route to the emergency room."

A.J. laughed in spite of herself. "Surely you jest," she admonished. "Tom's a friend of yours, and he knows that you're a friend of mine. I can't believe he would be that brutal."

"A reporter like Tom has no friends. And there's a very good reason why."

"But he seems to know everyone and everything."

"Not because he's interested or genuinely cares. He does it, A.J., because it's his business."

"He's the one who told you that Duke Carrington wanted to buy out the speedway, isn't he?"

"One and the same. And be aware, A.J., that anything Tom thinks Duke should know, you can be sure he'll divulge as soon as possible."

A.J. lowered her face into her hands. When she lifted her head again, she looked worried, her face weary and strained. Tears filled her eyes and threatened to overflow. That fact seemed to startle Jill.

"Hey, A.J., maybe I overstated Tom's style. I'm sorry if I rode you too hard about some things tonight. Don't take on like this. I'm sorry, hon."

"It's not you, Jill. I know that you love me and want the best for me. It's this business. The cut-throat racing industry. Sometimes, sometimes I absolutely hate it!"

"Then get out of it. Sell the speedway to Duke. Bank the money. Walk away from it. Do what you really want to do."

A.J. gave a bitter laugh. "At this point I don't know what that is."

"Go to college. Get into another career. Or do nothing for a while. Go to Florida and lay around on the beach. Live off the interest on the selling price for the Stacy legend."

Jill paused. "I'm giving up my career," she said, deftly changing the subject. "I had been planning on working after Rod and I got married. I even prepared a new resume. I was getting ready to apply for jobs for after the first of the new year."

"You're not going to?"

"Uh-uh. I realized that I'm tired of being a career woman, A.J. Unliberated and old-fashioned as it may seem, all I want to do is be a wife and mother. I want to be as perfect a helpmate to Rod as I can be. And I'm praying that we'll be able to start a family soon so that I can start raising our children to love the Lord. I want our children to be loyal to biblical teachings while doing their part to find answers for a troubled society."

"That's a pretty tall order, isn't it?" A.J. answered.

"Sure is," Jill agreed. "Being a mother takes a special kind of Christian commitment. I realize that now. And if God is good enough to bless Rod and me with a family, then the least I can do in grateful thanks is to be the best mother I can possibly be."

"And you will," A.J. assured her friend. "I have faith in that."

fifteen

The next month was chaotic, even though Dan had returned to take some of the burden from A.J.'s shoulders.

It had worked out well to have Sonny assist them at the speedway as they wrapped up the season's last stock car events. The elderly man had made many friends and was regarded as a legend in his own right. So when Dan had suggested that Sonny might consider returning for the next year's season, the retiree was quick to agree that working on a freelance basis would set well with him—and with his social security benefits.

Beth Carter, a widow, seemed almost giddy to realize that Sonny would be returning, and A.J. privately suspected that Beth was a major attraction at the speedway. A.J. had noticed that the older couple had enjoyed many evenings out when Sonny was in town.

Tom Findlay, realizing that Sonny wouldn't be around indefinitely, had made his interview top priority. The pictures were superb, and the feature printed in that issue of the *Daily News* was an account that made Sonny's local friends understandably proud.

Jill sent copies of the issue by express mail to Sonny, who had returned to his home for the off-season. Then she came by the speedway with a stack of papers fresh from the presses.

Quickly A.J. read the article, as did Beth who filched a crisp copy from the stack Jill had set on the counter. The older woman headed out the door to take it to Dan Barenfanger.

"You were wrong about Tom," A.J. told Jill. "I don't think he could have put together a nicer feature to honor Sonny. He'll be elated when he sees it."

"Believe me, A.J., I am delighted to be wrong. I only hope that I'm as wrong about you. And about Dan. Uh, I take it you haven't heard from your mother?"

"A birthday gift arrived."

"And your mother hasn't heard from you?"

A.J. gave Jill a long look. "I'm sure you know the answer to that one without having to ask."

"What are you waiting for, kid?" Jill whispered. "Now you're both alive, well, and have the capacity to talk. Pray God there doesn't come a day when you yearn to talk to your mother, to hear her voice one more time, and you find that you're parted by eternity."

"Mind your own business, not mine!" A.J. snapped.

Jill gave her a disgusted stare. "Why do you persist in being so foolish?" she snorted.

With that, in a rare show of pique, the reporter walked from the speedway office and slammed the door with a bang.

"What's eating her?" Dan asked when he entered.

"Oh, more or less a guy she works with," A.J.

explained evasively, "and the effect that he has on various people. Did you see the feature about Sonny? Jill just brought over a stack of extras of that issue."

"I sure did. I just tacked it up in the shop."

"Well, you're next, Danny Boy," A.J. informed him. "If he treats you as well as he did Sonny, then I'll allow myself to face-off with the notorious Tom Findlay. Jill claims he's a toughie. But judging from the article on Sonny, he's a pussycat. Jill had me half-afraid to go ahead with the interview."

"Tell the truth, and you'll have nothing to fear. The truth can set you free."

"That's going to be your M.O. for your session with Tom Findlay?"

Dan regarded her for a moment. "That's my M.O., as you call it, in daily life. I'm not a chatterbox," he explained, "so I don't run off at the mouth. When I have something to say, I say it. If I'm asked, I answer. But if I'm not asked, I tend not to talk. I don't get in trouble that way."

"Smart fellow," A.J. complimented, laughing.

"I'm a clean living person," Dan said. "And as far as I'm concerned, my life's an open book. If I tell the truth and Tom Findlay writes about it accurately, then any given reader's dislike over something is that individual's problem, not mine."

"Lucky you, Dan," A.J. said. "I should be so confident."

"You could be, if you really wanted to be, A.J. If you came to grips with your purpose in life and your relationship to the Lord, you would understand that what other people think of you doesn't matter a whit when you stack it against what the Lord thinks about you. All the public adulation in the world isn't worth a thing if you're not right with God. It's His approval and acceptance that's the most precious opinion in this world—and in the next."

"I'll try to remember that," A.J. dismissed. "Anyway, Tom wants to have an interview with you in two weeks," she switched the conversation to business. "We haven't scheduled my interview. We can work it out later. Maybe following one with Beth."

"As skittish as you are, you act like you have something to hide."

"Maybe sometimes I feel like I do," she admitted.

"If there are things in your life that bother you, A.J., turn the problems over to the Lord. No matter what it is, no matter what you've done, He can sort it out for you. He can forgive you even if you have a hard time forgiving yourself. And He can make a big problem seem awfully small when you trust in Him to handle it. He can make the most fearsome prospect easier to face when you're aware that you're not on your own. And He can give you the strength to accomplish things you wouldn't have believed yourself capable of on your own."

"Like David and Goliath?" A.J. suggested.

Dan looked surprised, but pleasantly so. "Been finding time to do a little reading, have you?"

A.J. smiled. "A little bit. It seemed the decent thing to do after Beth gave me that lovely, and very expensive, Bible for my birthday."

"She'll be glad to know that you're putting it to use. I know that I am."

"That makes it unanimous, I guess. Jill's cast her vote of approval, too. I'll have to keep trying to find the time to study."

"Jill will see that you do when she moves in with you after her lease expires."

"She's already warned me of that," A.J. said, laughing.

"When will she begin living with you?"

"Her lease is up in two weeks."

"You have only to say the word if you need help transporting items from her apartment to yours. Don't be shy about asking."

"We won't hesitate," A.J. said. "Thanks for offering. Maybe we can all go out for dinner afterward to celebrate."

Dan glanced at his watch. "It's supper time now. I haven't eaten, have you?"

"No."

"Then what do you say that we make a bee-line for Granny's Kitchen?"

"I say that that's the best idea I've heard all day."

"Then get ready for the best meal in town."

And the best company in the world, A.J. added mentally as Dan offered her his arm, and laughing, they exited the offices of Stacy Speedway.

sixteen

To A.J., the next two weeks seemed touched by magic. She saw as much of Dan outside speedway hours as she did when they were working together. Evenings, Jill frequently joined them. The house that Jill and Rod were having built was almost completed, so most of her belongings were being shipped there. But the trio exuberantly planned ahead for when they would move Jill's remaining possessions to A.J.'s large apartment.

Moving day arrived, and just as they had planned, they celebrated its completion with a great dinner at a nice restaurant.

"If we keep eating like this," Jill warned A.J., "neither one of us will fit into our dresses. Or we'll have to book an emergency appointment with the seamstress to let out our gowns as much as possible."

"Perish the thought," A.J. said.

"One thing good about our living together," Jill said, "is that we can police each other as the holiday meals and parties start appearing."

"Keeping your wedding in mind may make this the first Christmas in A.J. Stacy's history when she doesn't gain weight thanks to Beth Carter's chocolate walnut fudge."

"Your mother used to make a mean batch of chocolate caramels."

"Peanut brittle is my mother's specialty," Dan added, unaware that a tense moment had passed between the two women. "And she has big plans to make more this year. Dad said she'd asked him to get a candy thermometer to replace the one she accidentally broke during jam season."

"Not only do I want to look nice for your wedding, Jill," A.J. pointed out. "But I have to keep Tom's camera in mind, too. Alas, he'll be shooting pictures."

"And they say cameras don't lie," Jill said, "although I've seen some footage that makes me doubt the veracity of that old adage."

"Lucky me," Dan said. "I realize how fortunate I am listening to you weight-conscious females. I suppose more men worry about covering a bald spot than a spare tire."

"You don't have one of those, either, Mr. Barenfanger," Jill pointed out, taking a pinch of her ribs and frowning when she found more than an inch. "How do you do it?"

"Clean living and a pure heart," he teasingly replied.

"You'd better hope so when you face off with Tom Findlay," Jill warned.

Tom frowned. "That's what A.J. has been telling me. Is he really that bad?"

"Let's just say that he has a reputation. He's written some pretty dicey features. But let me also point out that the *Daily News* has not been sued because of him. Tom goes for all the news that's fit to print and occasionally dabbles in news that's not. But either way, the boy knows what he's doing. He makes sure of his facts, and if he thinks something's questionable, he runs it by our lawyers."

"I have nothing to hide," Dan said.

"Super. But a bit of friendly advice, Dan. Make sure you don't get tricked into telling anyone else's secrets. With Tom, think before you talk."

"I'll give that idea some thought," Dan agreed.

"When do you go face to face with the *Daily News*'s pride and joy?"

"The day after tomorrow."

"I'll say a prayer for you," Jill said.

"So will I," A.J. added.

"Hey, you girls have made me feel like perhaps I should put in a word to Beth to get her prayer partners involved."

"That's not a bad idea," Jill responded. "Where Tom Findlay's concerned, Dan, perhaps you should do just that."

Two days later, exactly on time, Tom Findlay arrived at the speedway. A.J., who had taken special pains with her makeup and attire, went out to meet him. She greeted him with exceptional warmth and then led him to the area where Dan generally worked.

They made small talk for a few minutes, then A.J. excused herself. "I'll leave you two to get on with your business. See you later, Dan," she said. "It was nice seeing you again, Tom. We loved the feature you did on Sonny. It was first rate."

A.J. returned to her office. The clock on the wall seemed to mock her.

One hour went by.

Then two.

"What on earth can they be discussing at such length?" she muttered, even though Beth had already gone home for the night.

When she considered how smooth Tom was at questioning and how open Dan could be, she felt a sinking sensation in her stomach.

Because Dan was open, honest, kindly, and compassionate, he generally assumed others were, too, unless he was proven wrong. A.J. hoped that Dan wasn't a man of principle being manipulated by a fellow with no ethics.

Two-and-a-half hours had gone by when she heard voices outside her door. The crunch of tires on gravel told her Tom had driven away. An instant later the office door swung open.

"How'd it go?" she asked.

"A piece of cake," Dan said. "We really hit it off. Tom Findlay's a nice guy. We ended up visiting more than we did interviewing and being interviewed. He's a wellspring of trivia and racing information. He's got a mind like a steel trap, and a really charming personality. I liked him a lot and enjoyed the time we spent together."

"Wonderful. Any of it off the record?"

"What?" Dan asked.

"You know, where you told him about it, but stipulated that it couldn't be printed," A.J. explained.

"Well, no," Dan admitted. "I didn't think about that. We were just talking. Tom's such a nice guy that I'm positive he won't use any of our private conversations in the article. He doesn't seem like that kind of guy at all."

As concerned as Dan suddenly looked, A.J. couldn't bear to make him feel worse. Yet she remembered all too well Jill's warning that Tom would try to soften subjects up by being charming and affable. After he got them to forget that they were conducting an interview, he would go for the jugular and let the subject bleed in public.

"Well, I'll be looking forward to seeing the article," A.J. said in a limp tone.

"Yeah. I will, too," Dan said, but suddenly without confident conviction.

Then quickly, almost upsettingly so, Dan Barenfanger said goodbye and left Stacy Speedway. It seemed as if he couldn't wait to get away. As if the Stacy property had become a scene of a crime that he hadn't realized he'd committed until it was too late.

A.J.'s heart sank. *What, oh what, could he possibly have told Tom Findlay?* she worried. *Did he have secrets from his past that could hurt him or the speedway?*

She knew that being the kind of man he was, Dan wouldn't intentionally hurt her—or anyone—for the world. Desperately, A.J. found herself praying that Dan Barenfanger's innocent, enthusiastic words and opinions wouldn't be twisted in such a way that they would blow apart the world of the people he'd quickly come to care about so much.

A.J. knew that if that happened, it would be almost more than Dan could bear.

And she realized that if he tarnished the Stacy legend or caused devastation to her carefully ordered world, it might be more than she could handle. If so, there was only one solution.

For the moment, A.J. couldn't even bear to consider having to follow through on that. She had trusted Dan. She had come to like him. Maybe now she even loved him. She was aware that sometimes their ideas and philosophies differed, even radically so. But while she certainly didn't require a yes-man, one thing she demanded from Dan Barenfanger: Over and above what love he had to give, he had to be as devoted to, and protective of, the Stacy legacy as she was.

seventeen

For the next week, the atmosphere at the speedway was tense. Going home at the end of the day brought no relief.

Jill was aware how worried A.J. was over Dan's interview. To ease her friend's stress, she tried to trivialize the possibilities, but behind her confident words and reassuring smiles, she feared how Tom Findlay might manipulate statements from the interview.

A.J. could sense her friend's true feelings, and while she was also afraid, she didn't know quite why. In some ways she felt as if she'd known Dan all her life. But when she stopped to think about it, she became aware of how little she actually knew about him. The idea that Tom might provide information that she'd find upsetting was an unpleasant specter.

A.J. also felt a ripple of concern that Dan might have made remarks that could be twisted or applied out of context, thereby making others look bad. Given the unusual silence Dan had maintained since the interview and the way he seemed to be avoiding her, A.J. realized that he was entertaining the same fears.

While A.J. would have loved for Jill to ease everyone's fears, there wasn't much her friend could do. She had not seen any drafts of the article and had no idea when it was going to be published.

"Tom hasn't said when it's going to run," Jill said when A.J. inquired for the third time. "Don't worry about it, A.J. You're probably concerned over nothing."

"I hope so," A.J. said.

"I have seen the contact sheets," Jill said, "and the pictures are superb."

"Of course. Dan's a very handsome man. That almost goes without saying. But it's not the pictures that have me worried."

"Nor me," Jill admitted with a tired sigh.

"I wish I'd never met Tom Findlay," A.J. muttered under her breath.

That evening, A.J. felt oddly restless. She couldn't concentrate on any of the small projects she wished to complete because of the conflicting thoughts that wrestled for control of her mind. She felt as if her mental circuits were about to overload.

Running her fingers through her hair, she gave herself a mental shake. "Why don't you work on something you have control over?" she asked herself out loud.

With fresh purpose, she took the gilt box of stationery from her desk and sat down. She reached for her favorite pen, composed her thoughts, and then began to write.

"Dear Mom," she began. "Thank you for the lovely birthday gift. You know me well to select something so perfect. But then, you should, right, because you're my mother. . . ."

It was difficult for A.J. to write to her mother after the long hiatus, but once the letter was begun, it seemed as if she recalled item after item of information or news to include. Forty-five minutes later the sheet was several pages long, and A.J.'s conscience was a great deal lighter.

"What are you doing, A.J.?" Jill asked. "You've been so quiet and busy."

"Just writing a letter."

"To anyone I know?"

"Yeah. My mom."

"Oh, A.J.," Jill whispered, hugging her. "I'm so glad."

"You're close to her, too, Jill. Want to add a few lines?" A.J. invited.

"I don't mind if I do," Jill said in a bright tone. "I guess you're aware that as an old family friend, your mother will be invited to the wedding?"

Actually, A.J. hadn't thought about wedding guests. But, it having been brought to her attention, she realized that it would have been rude for the Alexanders to exclude Liz Stacy from their celebration.

"Do you think she'll attend?" A.J. asked.

"I am sure she'd like to. And with a little encouragement from her daughter, I'm sure that she will. A.J., it's your chance. She could come for my wedding, you could see each other, and it might take the pressure off to have so many other people around. It wouldn't have the same stresses as if she traveled this far solely for a reunion."

Jill found a sheet of paper and sat down to zip

off a note to A.J.'s mother.

A.J. studied what she'd written, and then she picked up her pen again. "P.S. You probably figured out that I am one of the attendants at Jill's wedding in December. I know that it's a busy time, but I really hope that if you can get away you'll try to make it to the wedding. I'm sure you'll be receiving an invitation. It would be a wonderful opportunity to be together again. I know Daddy was very generous in the divorce settlement, but if you need a little help with travel expenses, please let me know, Mom, for I'd love to see you and wouldn't want something so insignificant to stand in the way."

A.J. reread the postscript just as Jill was folding up her note. "Read that and give me a critique, please," she asked Jill.

Her friend frowned as she scanned A.J.'s neat script. When she finished it, for a moment she didn't say anything.

"Well, what do you think?"

"I think those are the nicest words I've read all day! And those may be the nicest phrases your mother will feel that she's ever seen. I'm glad you're making this move, A.J. Any particular reason why?"

A.J. shrugged. "Somehow, the time simply felt right." She swallowed hard. "And I wanted my letter to reach her before the *Daily News* containing Tom Findlay's article about Dan can get to her and make the situation go from bad to worse."

"You're that worried about it?" Jill remarked.

A.J. nodded. "Dan's such an open and trusting man. Given that Dan was unaware that some answers should be kept off the record, if Tom Findlay led him down the right paths who knows what is going to appear in print!"

As each day's issue passed without the article's appearance, A.J. found her consternation rising.

Jill tried to relieve her friend's concerns by explaining the mechanics of column inches, copy to advertising space ratios, internal deadlines, and the like.

But A.J. wasn't mollified. "Do you know what I think is making it take all this time?" she blurted out.

"No. What?" Jill asked.

"Lawyers," A.J. dropped the bomb. "I think Tom Findlay has written such a poisonous treatment of Dan Barenfanger that it's having to be inspected by a team of legal eagles before it can be typeset and tossed onto the presses!"

"But that would be foolish to do," Jill reasoned. "After all, Tom hasn't done his interview with you. He'd know that if he ill-treats Dan, you wouldn't give him an interview."

"Maybe," A.J. agreed. "Unless he's doing what amounts to an unauthorized interview with me, using the material gleaned from Dan Barenfanger's impressions of his lady boss."

"Oh, A.J.," Jill murmured.

"Then that could happen?" she gasped. Jill's reaction dashed any hope A.J. had had that she was simply being an alarmist.

"Yes. A time or two he has done exactly that."

"What can I do?" A.J. asked.

"Trite as it may sound to you, pray. I will be," Jill said. "And you should ask Beth and her prayer partners. And Dan, if you're able to speak to him."

"Things between us haven't been very good. We're avoiding each other. I know we're both waiting to see what's printed so that we can discern what the situation is going to be when the dust settles."

The next morning, A.J. couldn't bring herself to admit to Beth how worried she was about the feature story on Dan. It seemed so petty to ask her to pray about it when A.J. only had her own suspicions that there was a problem.

A.J. had been in torment with each passing day, and Jill seemed to be unaware of when the article was going to run. So when Beth stepped out of the office, A.J. snatched up the receiver and dialed the offices of the *Daily News*. Instead of asking to be connected with Jill Alexander's extension, she cleared her throat and asked to speak with the editor.

Careful not to identify herself, A.J. said that she had heard there was going to be a feature on Dan Barenfanger. She explained that she wanted to be certain not to miss the issue and wished to be able to make arrangements to get extra copies.

"It's slated for this afternoon's issue, ma'am. It should be available around two o'clock. Thanks for your interest."

"Thank you for the information," A.J. responded

in a dazed tone when she realized that the waiting was almost over.

"I'm going out for a while, Beth," A.J. said as the older woman returned to the office. She hurried out the door before Beth could ask any troubling questions.

It was chilly outside, and the temperature and sky seemed to threaten snow. Shivering, A.J. slid into her white Corvette, grateful that the sun beaming through the sports car's windshield had created a toasty interior.

She inserted her key into the ignition, started the powerful car, and cruised from the parking lot. Dan heard her leave, stepped to the door, and waved.

A.J. gave a carefree tap on her horn and prayed once more that the world she and Dan Barenfanger knew could return to the climate they'd enjoyed the week before. She didn't want their working environment forever ruined by cold suspicion or hot and angry accusations of betrayal.

A.J. had a difficult time finding a parking slot near the newspaper's offices. She realized that she wasn't the only person interested in getting a copy of the *News* when it was hot off the presses.

She finally located a parking space two blocks away. She zipped into the empty space, locked the car up, and walked toward the *Daily News* property on shaky legs.

She was about to enter the lobby to purchase a paper when she spotted a curbside vending machine. Fumbling for her coin purse, A.J. was grateful that she could impersonally acquire a copy without having to encounter whoever was in charge of distributing the paper to customers. Neither would she risk running into Jill.

A.J. inserted the money, twisted the handle, and plucked a crisp, cool, faintly moist copy of the paper from the hefty stack. She glanced at the front page. The upper left-hand corner had a small photo of Dan and the legend, "Exclusive Interview!" Smaller print directed readers to the sports section.

A.J. fought down the desire to open the paper right there in the middle of the sidewalk. With quick steps, she walked back to her car. Even then, in easy sight of the *Daily News* building and with so many passersby, she didn't give in to her curiosity.

Quickly she started her engine, checked the mirror, zipped out into the street, and hung a right turn. Through her rearview mirror, she glimpsed a familiar black Thunderbird parking near the *Daily News* building.

A.J. drove aimlessly for a few blocks, then slammed to a halt curbside when she realized that she was near the park. Because of the cold weather, few people were taking advantage of the open spaces. A.J. realized that it would provide her ideal seclusion from prying eyes.

Her fingers shook and the paper seemed to resist her efforts to open it. Dan's grinning face was the first image she confronted. Her heart squeezed as she stared at his candid eyes. So open. So trusting. So handsome.

Drawing in a deep breath, A.J. began to read.

The first paragraph was innocuous.

The second was so-so.

By the third, her instincts were becoming alarmed.

By the fourth, she was outraged.

By the fifth, she was furious.

By the sixth paragraph, A.J. was openly weeping, and by the time she had reached the end of the article, she felt as if the pieces of her life had been held up for public inspection and ridicule.

Tom Findlay had not only wrecked her world, he had ruined any working relationship that A.J. and Dan could have hoped to have. The things Dan had said—as well as the things he had done and the associations he'd had—were nigh on unforgivable.

With a heavy heart, A.J. realized that she had only one choice.

With grim determination, she started her Corvette and drove back to the speedway. Dan's car was nowhere in sight. Neither was Beth's. For once, blessedly, Beth was gone, so A.J. set about the business of figuring up Dan's hours, his wages, and the necessary withholdings. Quickly she wrote out the check and tucked it into an envelope.

When A.J. heard tires crunch on the gravel she hoped that it was not Beth.

Luck was with her. It was Dan.

With a thundering heart, A.J. stood beside the door, waiting for him to alight. His face was strained. When he slammed the door of his T-bird she saw that he, too, had purchased a copy of the *News*. As pale as his features were, she knew that he had already read it. He would know exactly why she was so upset.

Closing her eyes in resolve, brushing away what tears lingered, she steeled herself to what had to be done.

A.J. wrenched the office door open.

Dan looked in her direction.

She rushed to him before he could say a word. Thrusting the envelope containing severance pay into his hand, A.J. announced with icy calm, "You're fired." Then she turned on her heel, dashed into the office, slammed the door, and locked it against any attempts to change her mind.

To his credit, Dan didn't try.

Ten minutes later, gravel crunched again. A.J. crossed to the window and saw Dan's black car disappear around a bend in the road. She would probably never see him again, and that thought brought a fresh torrent of tears.

That night, unable to bear going home, A.J. ordered a pizza to be delivered to her office. She ate without enjoyment. Then she took the phone off the hook, propped her feet on the corner of her desk, leaned back in the big swivel chair, and eventually fell into troubled, restless sleep.

eighteen

A cold gray light from the early morning sky was filtering into the office when pain from a crick in A.J.'s neck awakened her.

For a moment she looked around, dazed and disoriented. Then she recalled where she was, and why.

A.J. dropped her feet to the floor, leaned forward, and got up stiffly, rubbing the small of her back. She glanced at the clock and realized that Beth wouldn't be in for an hour. Jill wouldn't be leaving A.J.'s apartment for the newspaper until then, either. So A.J. would have to leave the office early enough to avoid Beth, and then use enough time going home so that she would be sure to miss Jill as well.

A.J. poured what coffee remained in the automatic pot that had been on overnight. It was thick as tar and strong enough to float a horseshoe. She took a sip, and the steaming, bitter brew seemed to revive her.

She turned on the radio, grateful for the dj's morning chatter for companionship as much as for the local and national news.

Eventually she shrugged into her jacket, retrieved her purse, and reached for Beth's pad of Post-It Notes.

"I won't be coming in today. A.J.," she wrote, and centered the note in the middle of Beth's neat desk.

She walked to the door, let herself out, and gulped

in a breath of frigid air.

Even though she'd slept all night—albeit poorly—
A.J. felt wretched and out of sorts. She intended to
go to her apartment, take the phone off the hook, and
collapse in bed. With any luck, she would be able to
sleep some more of her life away. It certainly was
too unpleasant to deal with right away.

When she unlocked her Corvette, A.J.'s eyes fell
to the tear-soaked issue of the previous day's paper.
It seemed to sit on the seat like a coiled cobra, ready
to poison her life if she so much as touched it again.

For fifteen minutes, she cruised aimlessly, then
she took a swing by her apartment building. Jill's
car was gone, so she nosed into a slot, glad she could
take refuge in her haven. A.J. collected the newspaper from her car and mentally consigned it to the
garbage pail. But when she entered her snug quar-
ters, she set the paper on the foyer table along with
her purse, and then slammed and locked the door.

She considered turning down the ringer on the
telephone and letting the answering machine take
any messages. That idea was nixed when she realized she'd probably be happier not hearing from
anyone. If people couldn't leave telephone messages
for her, she wouldn't have to deal with problems
until she felt like it.

A.J. took the phone off the hook. She went into
her bedroom and slipped off her clothes, pulling on
a soft flannel gown. Then she walked over to the
medicine cabinet in her bathroom and rummaged for
the sleeping pills her doctor had prescribed after her
father had died. She found the half-empty bottle,

took a pill, and crawled beneath the soft comforter of her bed.

It was a long time before A.J. fell asleep. Her chaotic thoughts prevented rest. Eventually the sleeping pill took effect, however, and she felt herself being pulled down into dreamless sleep.

She thought it was a dream—or a nightmare—when there was a battering on the bedroom door.

"Open up, A.J.! I know you're in there!" Jill said, pounding again.

A.J. threw back the covers, slid to the edge of the mattress, and fumbled into her slippers. She brushed her tangled hair away from her sleepy tear-swollen face as she opened the door to her temporary roommate.

"You look awful," Jill observed.

"Thanks. I feel awful, too."

The silence between the two women was strained. With a gentle touch Jill propelled A.J. toward the kitchenette. As they passed the phone, Jill returned the receiver to its cradle. Then she got down two coffee mugs and poured what remained in the pot left over from breakfast.

"Beth's called me several times. I told her I'd check on you during my lunch hour."

A.J. nodded.

"She tried to call but only got a busy signal—same as last night at the office. She was worried because you'd left a note that you wouldn't be in today. She's all by herself. Dan hasn't shown up, either."

"I know. I fired him. He won't be back."

"You what?" Jill gasped.

"Canned him. Sacked him. Pink-slipped him. Gave him his walking papers. Severed him. Whatever term you prefer."

"You're kidding."

"I assure you, I'm not."

"You can't even see how unfair you've been to him, can you?"

"Unfair!" A.J. cried, her voice a grating squall. "Jill, you work at the *Daily News*. You saw that article. And you have the audacity to call me unfair after what appeared in print? Get real!"

"Maybe you're the one who should get real, girl. Stop and think. Just how much of that article can actually be attributed to Dan? Precious little!"

"What do you mean?"

"What I mean, my dear, is that Dan wasn't the only source included in that feature. Obviously Tom was a busy boy—and a busy body—as he contacted old friends of the family, distant relatives, long-ago employees, racing enthusiasts, and anyone else who could be counted on to give a juicy quote about the Rick Stacy legend. Look and you'll see what I mean."

"It was bad enough reading it the first time. I'm not into masochism. I'm not going to read it a second time. I don't care what."

"Well, I care, and I'll read it to you!" Jill retorted.

She snatched up the offending issue, silently searching the article for important paragraphs. Then she rattled through the very worst quotes.

"Did Dan say that? Or that? Or that?" Jill cried in his defense. "No!" Jill answered her own question.

"He had no control over the sources who Tom contacted. And in all honesty, Tom shouldn't have run this purporting it to be an interview with Dan Barenfanger. What it amounted to was a smearing of the Stacy family, living and dead. And if it's any comfort, the switchboard operators at the paper have been fielding irate calls since the issue hit the streets."

"It's no comfort at all," A.J. said, even though there was a soothing element to be found in knowing of public dissatisfaction.

"I have received a number of calls at the office this morning," Jill said, "from people you know. They were concerned about how you might view their remarks. They, too, had no idea that Tom was going to use them as he did. And, unfortunately, they were naive and trusting enough that they didn't think to meet Tom's questions with 'No comment' or 'This is off the record.' "

"That's interesting."

"I thought so. You have a lot of friends, A.J., and at the moment, Tom has made an equal number of enemies. The editor and publisher are considering clipping Tom's news reporting wings. He's been warned that if another feature like this one goes through, he may be sending out resumes. This morning he got the word that the publisher himself wants to review Tom's future feature stories for content and treatment," Jill said. "Feel better?"

"Not really. It's too late now. At least for me," A.J. replied in a bleak tone.

"It's not too late. Dan hasn't left town yet," Jill

pointed out. "You could contact him, apologize, tell him that you realize it wasn't really his fault, and you could rehire him."

"No."

"No? What do you mean—no!"

"Exactly what I said: No! Nada. Uh-uh. Nope! Whichever word you prefer."

"In light of all the evidence, what's Dan done to offend you?"

"That's my concern, not yours."

"Something in this article has turned you off Dan like a dirty shirt," Jill said.

She began to speed-read her way through it. Abruptly, she threw the paper aside and stared at A.J. with open-mouthed incredulity.

"It's the Duke Carrington connection, isn't it?" Jill asked, stunned.

A.J. whirled on her. "Yes. Yes it is!" she cried, almost relieved to have it out.

"So anyone or anything that's ever come in contact with Duke Carrington is tainted as far as you're concerned? Maybe you should include me. I've known Duke and his family for years. A.J., he's a really nice guy. A decent person.

"Yes, he's made a few mistakes—at least as far as you're concerned. But do you really feel he'll never have done enough to atone for those mistakes? He can never pay enough of the debt to you to win your forgiveness? If that's the case, then I pity you, Amanda Jane Stacy, I truly pity you."

"I don't want your pity!" A.J. said in a hoarse, furious voice.

"You have it regardless. It's an emotion I feel for anyone who doesn't appreciate that to be forgiven we have to be able to forgive. Dan is hardly to be held to blame because he once worked for the Carringtons."

"It wasn't just any time when he worked for them. Check the paper, Jill, and you'll see the dates."

Silence spiraled as Jill rechecked the article. "So?"

"Doesn't that time period mean anything to you? Can you forget that easily?"

"Forget what?"

"When Kip died," A.J. said in an impatient tone. "Don't you see? Dan was heading up Duke Carrington's pit crew at the Indy 500 the year Kip was killed."

"So you're holding him responsible, too?"

"What do you think?" A.J. asked in a tight, tiny voice.

"I think that as obsessed as you are with laying blame, you'd probably hate the man who sold Duke Carrington fuel to run his racer that year. You'd hate the man who sold him his tires. You'd hate the man who—"

"That's not true!" A.J. shrieked.

"I should hope not. But I'm not convinced you don't feel that way." Jill glanced at her watch. "I've got to get back to the office. I'll be home for supper. I'll cook tonight. What do you want to eat?"

"Nothing."

"Aw, come on, you know you can't stay mad at me, A.J. Tell you what, I won't cook. I'll pick up something. Pizza—with olives—so we can extend each other peace."

The phone rang. A.J. glared at it. Jill scooped it up, answering pleasantly.

"Just a moment," she said in a sweet voice, "I'll get her."

Jill covered the mouthpiece.

"Your mom," she whispered. "She just got the *Daily News.* She sounds devastated. No matter how you feel right now, you be nice to your mother," she ordered. "You're not the only one hurt by this article. She didn't look so good, either."

nineteen

A.J. was sitting in her dark apartment, swaddled in a fleecy full-length bathrobe and slippers, when Jill inserted her key in the lock that evening.

"A.J.?" she called out when she stepped inside, fumbling for the switch for the hanging lamp in the foyer. "Are you home?"

"Over here," A.J. said from the corner chair near the electric fireplace.

"I saw your car was still in the lot," Jill said. She shot A.J. a glance. A.J. turned away, knowing how awful she looked. Her cheeks were swollen from crying and her eyes felt raw and red, irritated by grit every time she blinked. "So how'd the call from your mother go?"

"Okay."

"How is she?"

"Devastated."

"I figured as much. When I got back to work this afternoon, I gave Tom Findlay a piece of my mind. I let him know what I thought of his journalistic ideals and personal ethics." Jill paused. "I guess the article upset her, huh?"

"It arrived in Mom's mail this morning. But she got calls from friends last night. One friend here in town called her and was so upset that she was crying. She was afraid that my mother would never speak to her again after how Tom used what

157

she'd said in the worst possible manner."

"Your mother wasn't furious?"

"Not any more than anyone would've been. She was more concerned about me that she was worried about herself."

"Mothers are like that," Jill murmured.

"I suppose so."

"So things went pretty well for you?"

"Ummm. The only thing bad, I guess, will be Mom's phone bill when she gets it," A.J. made a weak joke. "We talked for over an hour. Daytime rates."

"A bargain at almost any price," Jill decided.

"I'm glad that my letter to her arrived before she got the newspaper."

"That probably gave her the courage to call you."

"Yeah," A.J. agreed. "Otherwise she probably wouldn't have dared."

"If nothing else comes of this horrible situation, at least we can consider it a blessing that it's brought you and your mother together again. Maybe you can start rebuilding some of those bridges that were burned in the past."

"She's planning on coming here for the wedding."

"Super," Jill said.

"I can tell that she's anxious to see me."

"And—"

"Okay, I'll admit it. I'm really looking forward to seeing Mom again."

"I'm so glad. I've prayed for this to all work out."

A.J. paused. "Mom." She repeated the word, savoring it like a sweet confection on her tongue. "For the past several years I've felt as if I didn't have a mother. I've felt like an orphan."

"And I know what pain it was to your mother to be in a retirement community where her friends were bragging about their grandchildren, and she hadn't even a daughter to claim."

"I think we've changed all that," A.J. said. "I invited her to stay with me when she comes to town."

"I wouldn't have it any other way. Beth will be glad to know that you and Liz have mended fences," Jill said, "Now the one person remaining to communicate with is Dan."

"No way," A.J. said.

Jill groaned. "Don't go getting obstinate on me, A.J. Sometimes you are so mulish."

"I've been thinking a lot this afternoon," she responded decisively. "Dan had any number of opportunities to tell me about his link to Duke Carrington."

"From what I read in that article, Dan's had links to any number of America's racing families, knowing some better than others. And he tends to be a bit taciturn. He's not the type to try to impress you by name-dropping."

"He had to have known what Duke Carrington's name means to me."

"Why? Only those of us really close to you—or close to Duke—are aware of your obsession."

"Would you please quit calling it that?" A.J. snapped.

"I calls 'em as I sees 'em, my dear," Jill retorted. "On this matter—and in a few other race-related areas—you most certainly are obsessed. But back to the point: Why should Dan have known? In the past few years he probably wasn't that close to Duke. Remember, Dan had moved to another state. It wasn't until recently that Dan's had a close association with Stacy Speedway. If he detected how you felt then, A.J., he probably felt it smart to keep his mouth shut."

"I feel betrayed," she answered bleakly.

"You would," Jill grumped. "Because you're obsessed."

"You're obsessed with labeling me obsessed. But I think that we can agree on the point that thanks to Dan's comments in that article, the whole world now knows that Duke Carrington would like to buy Stacy Speedway."

"That's not a news-breaking statement, A.J.," Jill said. "Anyone with a heartbeat and discernible brain activity could have figured that one out. Stacy Speedway represents a going business, a thriving racetrack. It has a solid record, and it would be a safe investment. It isn't chancy—like trying to build a racetrack from the ground up as your father did years ago.

"Of course Duke would be interested in buying it. There probably aren't that many tracks of Stacy Speedway quality around. And then there's the little fact that Duke's oldest boy, who recently got married and is in the family business, might like something to turn his attention to in order to expand the Carrington holdings."

"I suppose that's true. But they can look else-where. I'm not interested."

"Maybe you should be."

"This is beginning to sound repetitious," A.J. warned.

"Then at risk of becoming redundant, I shall continue with my points of logic," Jill said, and segued into convincing reasons why A.J. should consider divesting herself of the speedway. "I know that Dan shares my feelings."

Instead of striking a chord, Jill's comment caused A.J. to react as if nails were raking across a black-board.

"Oh, I'm very sure of that. He showed up on the doorstep of Stacy Speedway, looking for a job, seeming tailor-made for the position. I was so impressed I didn't check references or look into his work background. So I didn't discover the Carrington connection, which would have been revealed at the outset had my suspicions been aroused."

"So? So what?"

"So that makes me wonder if I wasn't being flim-flammed."

"Are you serious?"

"I've never been more earnest. It was about that time that your Tom Findlay asked if I was going to sell the speedway to Duke Carrington. If Duke couldn't get me to sell by making an offer to our law firm, perhaps he hoped that he could plant someone on the inside to make it happen."

Jill stared. "I can't believe what I'm hearing."

"I wouldn't either, Jill, except that I've lived it. You know about the problems I had at that one race. Well, Duke Carrington wasn't near the car. That I know. But he wouldn't have to be if his old mechanic had become my mechanic and was sabotaging from within."

"You are so wrong," Jill said flatly. "A.J., you have absolutely no comprehension of just how wrong you are. Dan would never, never do something like that."

"How do you know?" she retorted.

"Because he's a committed Christian and an example to other believers. He wouldn't do that to you, A.J., nor disappoint the Lord through such devious, manipulative, unethical behavior."

"You have your views, and I have mine. The subject is officially closed."

And it remained that way.

The subject was not raised when A.J. spent the Thanksgiving holiday with Jill, her family, and her fiancé.

A.J. didn't rise to the bait when Jill informed her that Dan had sublet his apartment and moved away. He was living nearer his parents to help his father with his business.

"I don't want to hear about Dan!" A.J. said in a hot tone.

"I think you're a liar," Jill said, laughing softly. "As betrayed as you feel, I still think you're mad as blue blazes because Dan hasn't come around on bended knee, seeking your forgiveness for offenses he never committed. Without that, you can't be the grand lady and absolve him."

"I'm warning you!" A.J. sputtered furiously.

"You're crazy about him," Jill teased. "Without Dan around, you're miserable, but you're too proud to admit it. You know that you treated him unfairly, but your pride's getting in the way of turning the situation around. All it would take is a phone call or an apologetic letter, and Dan would be back working for you, happy as if he'd never left. Left? I stand corrected: been driven away!"

"Maybe I don't want him back!" A.J. flared.

"You can say that, A.J. Stacy, but even you don't believe it. You came to care about Dan the way you've never felt for any other guy."

"So what?" A.J. cried, giving way to tears. "So what if I did? It doesn't make any difference how I felt because Dan Barenfanger doesn't care about me at all."

"That's what you think?" Jill asked.

"That's what I know."

"Then you're as wrong about that as you are about so many other things."

A.J. lifted her face and wiped her eyes. Even though she had told herself that the feelings were dead, a stubborn little shoot of hope blossomed in her heart.

"What do you mean?"

"Dan thinks the world of you, A.J. He thinks you're quite a girl. He'd ask you out, like he did once, except—"

"Except what?"

"Well, except that you're not a committed Christian. You're not a believer. As much as you have in common, A.J., he knows that without shared faith in Christ you'd have nothing to join you together in a strong, enduring relationship."

"Perhaps his mother can find someone suitable," A.J. snapped, flouncing from the living room. Jill's heavy sigh seemed to follow after her, an echo of her own unhappiness.

"Give Dan a call, huh?" Jill suggested through A.J's closed bedroom door. "I've got his number on my Rolodex. I'll get it for you. I'll even dial the number on your behalf. I'll pay for the call. I'll—"

"Never," A.J. muttered through gritted teeth. "Never!"

twenty

The day before Jill and Rod's wedding, A.J. drove to the airport to meet her mother. She was nervous as she moved through the heavy traffic. She arrived early, found a parking slot, then went into the terminal to wait.

To her relief, the nonstop flight was on time. A.J. proceeded directly to the green concourse and selected a seat with a clear view through the massive windows. That way she could see the airplane bearing her mother come roaring in.

Five minutes later, the airplane came into sight. Other people who awaited the arrival of loved ones clustered near the windows. As a steady stream of passengers walked down the steps and across the tarmac toward the entrance to the terminal building, those who waited broke away from the clustering crowd to go meet them.

A lump filled A.J.'s throat when she caught sight of her mother, the first glimpse she'd had of her in years. Jill was right. Her mother was fit, trim, and Florida tan. But she'd also aged, and A.J. realized that a few of the new wrinkles her mother wore had probably been put there because of her behavior.

She was almost overwhelmed by sadness when she considered the years that had slipped by— years that were now impossible to regain. Tears

pricked A.J.'s eyes. She moved toward her mother
as the small woman stepped through the door into
the terminal.

Liz Stacy's eyes searched the crowd. They connected with her daughter's tear-filled eyes. She
followed the other passengers until the steel railing no longer parted her from her A.J.

Liz fell into A.J.'s outstretched arms and heard
her daughter cry, "Oh, Mama!"

"My baby," Liz crooned, hugging A.J., patting
her shoulder, bussing her cheek. "Our little Indy
Girl!"

Suddenly A.J. realized that Indy Girl had been
the family's pet name for her for as long as she
could remember. As a result, she had always
thought of herself in terms of the Stacy legend.
She had never been able to imagine any other
destiny for herself.

As she led her mother to the car and listened
intently on one level, A.J. was silently wondering
if she really wanted to compete in the Indy 500.
Was her dream, instead, simply the result of her
desire not to disappoint her family?

"So how are your plans to make the Indy going?" Liz Stacy asked in a bright tone. Behind her
carefully smiling eyes lurked the raw fear that
she'd lose A.J. to speed, just as she had the rest of
her family.

"Okay," A.J. said. Hesitantly, she added, "But
I'm not sure I'm going to take a shot at it, Mom. I,
well, there are other things in life. At least that's
what I've been told," she added ruefully. "At age

twenty-seven, maybe it's time for me to do some exploring of uncharted territory and find out if it's true that there could be another purpose for my life."

"The racing life is a demanding one," Liz said. "It can ask a price higher than you're one day willing to pay. To be frank, darling, I don't want that for you. And I know that your father wouldn't, either."

In a broken tone, Liz described what racing had done to her, to the family she loved, and to the man she adored. She had realized that while her husband cared for her, he cared about racing more. At the time, she had felt she had no choice but to leave, painful as that decision had been.

"As you know, your father and I stayed in touch," Liz said softly. "As age began to creep up on Rick, he began to realize what his career had cost us. He flew down to see me several times. What you don't know is that your father and I were on the verge of reconciliation and remarriage when he was killed."

"Mother!" A.J. gasped. "I had no idea."

"Sad but true," Liz said. "His plans were to move to Florida where I now live. He liked the area, a beautiful retirement community that also has plenty of opportunity for the younger generation. There were several colleges in the area that you could have gone to, A.J. We could have been a family again."

"But the business?" A.J. reminded. She was thinking of the speedway first, and she suddenly realized that she always did.

"He was going to sell it," Liz murmured. "To Duke Carrington, if Mr. Carrington wished to buy it. Rick was going to contact him with a proposition that would have allowed us a divestiture and given Duke a hand up in the racing industry."

"What!" A.J. gasped.

"It's true. Your father had so many plans, if only he'd lived to carry them out. I begged him not to race in the last few competitions he had scheduled. With such happy plans in the works, he risked so much. I pleaded with him to walk away. But he was so sure that his luck would hold. Then he died, and all of the plans we had to become a family again passed away with him."

"Oh, Mom."

A.J.'s mother began to weep into a linen handkerchief. "I cherished Rick Stacy as a young girl, I adored him as his wife, and I still love him as a retired ex-wife. If only things could have been different. But I must accept it and simply hope and pray for the future of our family."

"Mama, why didn't you tell me all of these things?" A.J. cried in a soft, pain-filled voice.

"I tried to. I wanted to," Liz replied. "But at the time of your father's death, you weren't able to listen. Or you weren't willing to understand what I was saying. Or maybe you thought that I was making it up to salve my own conscience."

"I don't even remember trying to discuss the business," A.J. admitted. "But then I was so numb with grief that I know I was blocking out reality. I didn't allow myself to see or hear anything or in any way become more vulnerable."

"And after the funeral and the settling of the estate," Liz recalled, "to my agony, I found that we weren't on speaking terms. I felt that your blame for my marriage disintegrating deepened. That you were certain if I hadn't left, the disasters that followed would not have happened. I felt that you believed the situation was entirely my fault."

"For that, Mother, I am sorry. Truly sorry. More than you'll ever realize. I never saw what it was like for you."

"I appreciate your apology, honey. But I want you to know that I forgave you a long time ago. And I have prayed that you would someday forgive me for any grievances that I've accidentally or thoughtlessly caused you to suffer."

As Liz Stacy fell silent, A.J. reached across and patted her arm. At last, A.J. understood the conflicts that had eventually caused her mother and father's divorce. She also realized why an aging Rick Stacy had walked around the speedway office grumping that Stacy Speedway owned him and was a relentless, merciless taskmaster.

A.J., who had unsuspectingly fallen under the speedway's spell, in the same way found herself a prisoner to its demands. She had experienced the melodramatic reality her father had spoken of as the racing industry claimed him body and soul. Was it about to own her in the exact same way?

She hoped that she wouldn't look back like her father and feel that racing had cost her all that she valued, all that she wanted from life. She shuddered when she realized that it could extract the ultimate of her as it had of Kip and her father. All her happy plans for bright tomorrows could easily vanish between one heartbeat and the next.

Her father had reached a point where he was trying to find solutions that would allow him to walk away from racing, and A.J. felt herself fast moving toward that same juncture, speeding toward a point of no return.

There had been private moments—several of them recently—when A.J. had wanted to simply wake up a normal woman, not a racing industry business executive. She'd thought about being the woman some man cared about, instead of always being spotlighted as the Indy Girl.

Rick Stacy hadn't listened to reason, A.J. realized. It was up to her to find the will to turn away. The path she was following had become, just as Jill Alexander had warned, an obsessive, all-consuming goal.

A.J. didn't know if she had the self-control it took to give up all her deeply ingrained goals. But Dan Barenfanger had assured her that with God's help all things were possible.

She'd recently dared to approach God in prayer, seeking help for other people. Now was the time, she realized, for A.J. Stacy to plead with the Lord on her own behalf.

twenty-one

Following lunch at a cozy, downtown restaurant, A.J. drove her mother to the home of a family friend. Liz Stacy had been invited to stay there that night because of the confusion the wedding preparations had brought to A.J.'s apartment. After Jill's wedding the next day, Liz planned on spending several days with A.J. before returning to Florida.

A.J. was surprised to discover that bridesmaids could be kept as busy as the bride on the day before the wedding. After dropping off her mother, she was kept scurrying about the city, a zip of flashing white on the street. She drove from one specialty shop to another, taking care of last-minute errands for Jill.

By the time she met the rest of the wedding party outside the church for the wedding rehearsal, A.J. felt limp. The pastor arrived and ushered everyone into the sanctuary. There he explained the importance of the occasion and pointed out the symbolism of the ceremony. He carefully explained the individual responsibilities each member of the wedding party would have the next day.

When the rehearsal was completed, Rod's family took everyone out for a traditional groom's dinner.

"Someday it'll be your turn, A.J.," Jill said when they were in the powder room at the restaurant.

"Maybe. Maybe not," A.J. said. "Perhaps I'll simply be always the bridesmaid, but never the bride."

"I don't think so," Jill said.

A.J. saw a twinkle in Jill's eyes that seemed to suggest that the recently resigned reporter knew something that she, A.J. Stacy, did not.

"I'll see you at the apartment," A.J. said. "I haven't shown my face at the speedway all day."

"Call the *Guinness Book* people," Jill teased. "This must be a first."

"I think it is," A.J. said. "I haven't even given the business a thought."

"See?" Jill teased. "And you actually lived to tell about it. There is life-after-speedway, isn't there?"

"It appears there could be. But I guess I'm addicted to it. Even though I told Beth I wouldn't be in at all, I feel compelled to check the mail, consult the answering machine, and see if Beth has Post-It Notes marching up my desk blotter."

"Drive carefully, A.J.," Jill said when they stepped outside. "It feels like it's spitting sleet. Or something."

"You're warning the Indy Girl to drive carefully?" A.J. teased. "Bite your tongue."

"Don't argue. Just do it. I'll see you soon. I'll make hot chocolate, and we can talk long into the night."

"Sounds good. But we won't stay up too late."

"Right. We both want to look our best tomorrow," Jill agreed.

Once more she gave A.J. a funny look. A.J. was convinced her friend had a secret, but from long experience, she knew Jill wouldn't let her know anything about it until she thought the time was right.

The sky was heavy, and the temperature hovered at the freezing mark. A.J. turned on her windshield wipers, and they pushed the snow and rain around on the windshield. As the Corvette's defroster kicked on in full force, the warmth blowing on the windshield helped the wipers deal with the slushy precipitation that peppered down.

It was actually a beautiful, ethereal sight, A.J. realized as she turned into the brightly lit Stacy Speedway. The beam of the security light illuminated the ribbonlike streams of snow and ice.

While it was pretty to look at, it was not pleasant to deal with, and A.J. let out a squeak when her dress shoes almost gave out from under her as she stepped from her car to the sidewalk.

Cautiously she made her way to the office and let herself in. She went through the mail. There was nothing that couldn't wait. She glanced at the Post-It Notes. Again, nothing that couldn't be postponed until after the weekend.

The red dot on the answering machine offered a steady glow. No calls to return, either.

A.J. was about to exit her office when she heard a sharp sound ring out from the shop area.

Her heart momentarily stopped beating, then it raced to a thundering pulse as she wondered what—and who—it could be.

For a moment she considered the folly of apprehending an intruder. But when another bang rang out from the area that no one had used since Dan Barenfanger's dismissal, curiosity triumphed over caution. A.J. made her way as swiftly as she could to the shop area.

She tried the door. It was locked. She fumbled for her set of keys and found the right one. Whoever was inside was so engrossed that her attempts to unlock the door went unnoticed.

Quietly A.J. let herself in.

She stood, stunned. Dan Barenfanger was working on Rick Stacy's racer!

A kaleidoscope of emotions washed over her. She realized how much she'd missed Dan since she'd fired him. And she realized how infuriated she was to find him back on the premises without her permission.

She didn't bother to sort out her conflicting emotions. Instead she confronted him, her voice hot and hostile.

"Just what do you think you're doing here? How did you get in here?" Disappointment raked across her soul. She had believed Dan was honest, yet apparently he had been sly enough to have made a duplicate set of keys to the shop while he worked at the speedway.

"Beth let me in," Dan said, not stopping his labor. "She knows I'm here."

"Well I didn't. And I'll take that up with her first thing Monday morning!"

"She was only doing what she felt was best. For you."

"Right," A.J. said and gave a bitter laugh. "What do you think you are doing working on my father's racer?"

"Attending to unfinished business, Miss Stacy. That's what I'm doing."

"Your business at Stacy Speedway ended quite abruptly, as I recall, and some time ago, too. You have no business here now."

"I'm afraid I do. It's part of my mission in life," Dan said. "My mission to keep race drivers—and that includes you—safe."

A.J. was left speechless.

In a quiet voice Dan explained that when he'd been going over the racer the last time, he'd seen a part that didn't look one hundred percent right to him. There was nothing he could specifically identify as being out of place, but he sensed there was a problem. He had looked the part over carefully and had had no choice but to put it back on. Replacements for the piece took a long time to arrive. But he had made a note to order a replacement part because his instincts told him that the current one had not been as well fabricated as quality control inspectors demand.

"Something about the piece told me it was ready to fail under the stress of racing, A.J.," Dan explained. "I was going to replace it, but before I could, you fired me."

"But, Dan, that's . . . I . . . I. . . ." A.J. stuttered, touched, in spite of her sudden flash of anger.

"I ordered the part and took delivery of it at Mom and Dad's house where I'm living for the time being. I knew that it would arrive in time for me to be able to put it on when I came back to town for Jill and Rod's wedding. Beth had said she'd let me in so I could do it late at night. That way you'd never know."

"That Beth!" A.J. sighed under her breath.

"I'm sorry you found out," Dan said. "But there was no way that I could have lived with myself knowing that you were driving a racer that could malfunction at any moment. It would have been like sentencing you to compete behind the wheel of a ticking time bomb."

"You did that for me, Dan?" A.J. whispered, her voice tremulous when she realized how much he must care in order to go to all the trouble that he had. Her heart softened.

"It's my mission in life, remember, Miss Stacy?" he asked. "I recall once upon a time telling you all about it."

To A.J., his voice seemed mocking. The warmth she'd felt at the hope that Dan cared for her and might love her disappeared in the chill of rejection.

A.J. turned away.

"I'll have Beth send you a check for the part and your labor," she offered, trying to retain her composure as she retreated toward the night's darkness.

"See you at the wedding tomorrow," Dan said.

A.J. didn't dare to reply. She couldn't. She was too choked up with bitter tears. A hiccupping sob escaped her when she stepped outside, and her hot tears mingled with the cold sleet slashing the silken skin on her cheeks.

She bent into the gathering wind and rushed to her car. Her hair hung in damp strands against her face as she leaned forward to start the engine. Turning out of the parking lot, she saw Dan's Thunderbird tucked away close to the side of the building, and she understood why she hadn't noticed it when she'd driven into the speedway.

Thoughts and impressions swirled through A.J.'s mind as she automatically headed toward home. Her Corvette fishtailed on the highway when she left the speedway's frontage road. Although driving conditions were bad, A.J. realized she should take time to think before she got back to the apartment. She needed to have her troubled emotions under control before she faced Jill and her reporter's gift for asking direct and painfully probing questions.

As A.J. thought about the manner in which she had fired Dan, she finally recognized that she had ill-treated him. He hadn't said a word in his defense. She had been horribly unfair to him, but he hadn't offered a complaint to her face. She knew that he had also said only the kindest things about her to the people who knew them both. She had found him guilty by his mere associations with people she had held grudges against, again, unfairly. While Dan had had every right to rail against his unfair dismissal, he had chosen to be silent.

Tears filled A.J.'s eyes until she could hardly see. She brushed them away with one hand while driving with the other, squinting to make out the country road that rimmed the very edge of the city and would lead to her apartment on the far side of town.

A.J. realized that she had to apologize to Dan when she saw him again. She was stung by all the mistakes she had made, and she was shamed by the knowledge that although she had been so hateful to Dan, he still cared for her.

After what she had done, a normal man wouldn't care if she drove a racer with a weakened part. In fact, most men might laugh over it as a private joke. They would think that if someday the part killed her, it would be good enough for a lady boss like A.J. Stacy.

But not Dan. He wanted her to live on, to live on long enough to know the Lord as he did. So it became his mission to save her life, trusting that God would save her soul.

A.J. cried harder when she realized the opportunity she had missed. Dan who wanted to love a Christian woman, one with whom he would be equally yoked. Dan who had been such a good friend. Dan who had been a confidant. Dan who had once so thrillingly kissed her. Dan, who had taken to calling her sweetheart—a soft word that had pierced straight to her woman's heart, making her feel cherished, loved, cared for.

But now, he had made his point clear. She was Miss Stacy. To him the affection was gone, replaced by a relationship that was all business.

Well, even if he no longer cared for her, the first chance she got, she was going to apologize to him for all her errors. And she was going to do something even more important after she and Jill had retired to their rooms for the night.

Before she went to sleep she was going to pray to God and ask Him to forgive her for doing the thoughtless, vengeful, selfish things she had done. There were so many things she was sure she couldn't remember them all.

A.J. gripped the steering wheel and drove over the hilly, curving route that skirted the river along the edge of town. She was aware, as never before, of just how self-centered her existence had been, how often she had gone against God's will and followed her own headstrong desires.

There were a lot of people who would be receiving apologies from her, she realized. But before she could go to them, she had to ask God to forgive her and to guide her so that she might do His will. Only He could give her the strength to abandon her own desires when they were not part of His plan.

Just as A.J. was starting to feel the confidence that comes from a plan of action, the car suddenly went out of control on an icy curve.

Wrestling the light, fiberglass vehicle on the narrow road, A.J. knew terror. She sagged with relief when she believed she had brought the car under control, but just then, it spun away from her and went sliding into a grassy, sleet-covered berth between the road and the river.

A.J. got out of her car, looked around, and decided that she had been in worse predicaments and managed to drive her way out. She glanced toward the sharp drop off to the river. The black ribbon of water reflected the glow of her car's lights. She knew the river wasn't terribly deep except during spring runoff. There were fallen trees, snags, and beaver lodges on it, but the current was not swift.

She felt that with her car's power she could drive her way from the soft, grassy area and get back onto the road. The friction from her tires would melt the ice crystals clinging to the grass, and soon she would be home having warm cocoa with Jill.

A.J. got back into the car but neglected to snap on her seat belt. Putting the car in gear, she gripped the wheel and tapped the accelerator. The tires spun and the rear end of the car veered to one side. A.J. countered that movement automatically, and then remembered the racers' advice: When in doubt, pour on the power. So often in racing speed and power could mean the difference between success and disaster.

A.J. gave it all she had. The tires screamed. The Corvette moved ahead sluggishly, slipping from side to side. But A.J. could see that she was making headway.

She was already envisioning success when suddenly there was a dull, muffled roar. The earth shifted. The headlights flashed an arc across the leaden sky. A.J. was thrown across the car, and the Corvette flipped end over end, coming to rest on its side.

When the terrifying moment ended, A.J. assessed her situation. Cold river water was seeping in around her. As mud balls landed on what had been her pristine white car, she realized what had happened. The sodden bank that had looked so solid from the driver's seat of her car had actually been eaten away and undercut. The weight of her car had been more than it could hold. The bank had collapsed into the river.

A.J. began to laugh ruefully. Once more her impetuousness and determination to take care of herself had landed her in a jam. She should have walked to where help could be had and let professionals at rescuing troubled drivers do it their way.

But no. She, A.J. Stacy, the cocky, know-it-all Indy Girl, had had to ride it out on her own. And once more, she had done it all wrong.

One hour passed.

Then another.

A.J. began to sob when she realized how helplessly she was trapped. What if Jill assumed she had decided to sleep at the office? What if Jill had dozed off without realizing that A.J. had not come back to the apartment? What if no one was aware that she was missing?

The river lapped against her car. Icy water came

up to A.J.'s chest, and the passenger door she had landed against was pinned shut. By what? A log that was holding her car, keeping it from washing downriver into deeper water?

A.J. had heard the roaring thud of dirt mound high against the driver's door, preventing escape through that avenue. She didn't want to kick out the windshield—yet—but the rear glass was too tiny for her to hope to escape through.

A.J. was afraid to move. With the wrong motion, the car could be dislodged and move down the river. More earth could avalanche down on her.

Shivering uncontrollably, A.J. was as miserable and frightened as she'd ever been in her life. Hot tears rolled down her cheeks as sleet began to fall even harder.

With each moment that passed, A.J. realized that she might not be rescued at all. She could drown or die of exposure. If the temperature plummeted and a midwestern blizzard roared through, she could be frozen to death by the time her body was found.

A.J. knew that she couldn't wait until she was home in her room to talk with God. She had to do it now. She thought through her life, remembering the good and the bad. There were situations that caused her acute regret. Other incidents filled her with warmth as she recognized the caring hand of God protecting her.

She was thankful that her relationship with her mother had been healed. Whatever the outcome of her current situation, A.J. knew her mother wouldn't have to face tragedy without knowing how much her daughter loved her.

Although A.J. wanted to live, for the first time she realized how her life was in God's hands. Her destiny was His to determine.

"Not my will, Lord, but yours," she whispered, praying to be rescued.

A.J. stared into the inky dark. The windshield was thick and frosty with gathering ice, but A.J. felt peace. She trusted that her Lord and Savior would send her the help she needed.

She wasn't sure how much more time passed, but suddenly she heard the sound of engines up near the roadway. One passed by, then another.

A.J. cried out for help, but no one slowed down. She was left alone in frozen silence once more. A.J. thought she was dreaming when, about fifteen minutes later, an engine rolled slowly along, then halted. The beam of a flashlight crisscrossed, then lit up the ice-covered windshield.

"She's down there!" A.J. recognized Dan's voice calling out. "Send for a wrecker!"

A moment later, A.J. was startled by Dan's presence on the hood of her Corvette.

"A.J., can you answer me?" he asked. "Are you okay?"

"I can hear you," she said. "And except for being cold and trapped, I . . . I'm fine."

"Super, sweetheart," Dan said. "Don't worry. We'll have you out of there in no time. My dad's got a gas station and runs a wrecker. I've been

back in business with him since I left the speedway. I'm an old hand at this kind of work. I'll set
up the cables myself."

"Thank You, God," A.J. whispered.

Then she began to cry. From relief. And because
Dan Barenfanger had just called her sweetheart.

As good as his word, the help Dan had promised
arrived within minutes. A.J. heard the clatter of
Dan setting chains and cables into the correct
position.

"We'll have to haul you up, hon," Dan said, "but
from here on out it's a piece of cake. Just close
your eyes and pretend you're in an elevator. When
I open the door, you can step out."

One minute passed. Then two.

The wrecker's winch whined.

Mud sucked at A.J.'s car. Branches from the tree
scratched at the crumpled fiberglass body. Then
A.J. felt the car being lifted up and swung toward
solid ground and safety. The passenger door
opened and A.J. fell into Dan's warm arms.

Cheers went up as Dan held A.J. He cupped his
hand under her chin, lifting her lips to his. In her
kiss, she thanked him for rescuing her, thanked
him for being the kind of man he was, and thanked
him for praying for her.

"I'm sorry that I fired you, Dan. It was horrible
of me to strike out at you because of my own
feelings. Can you forgive me?"

"I already have. Long before now."

"I should've known that you would," A.J. said
softly.

"Anyway, I knew at the time you really didn't mean it. We do sometimes tend to hurt most the very people we love."

"Then you knew that I loved you?"

"Uh-huh, sweetheart. I figured it out long before you did. You sent me away. But I knew that God would bring me back."

"And He has returned you to me."

"To a woman who's everything I want in a wife."

"A Christian woman," she sighed, "who very much wants to have a career change."

"You're giving up racing?"

"As of several hours ago, Dan. Now I'll have to find something else that I'm qualified to do and find myself a new career."

"Can a guy who loves you offer suggestions?"

"Sure," A.J. said.

"How does it sound to be married to a grease-monkey, gas-pumping, wrecker-driving guy who loves you?"

"Sounds super," A.J. purred from the circle of her arms, and gave him a light kiss when she found his smiling lips absolutely irresistible.

"The pay's not so great," he warned.

"But the benefits," A.J. said softly, "are going to be absolutely out of this world."

"You're interested in the position?" Dan teased.

"Uh-huh."

"Then the answer is yes?" Dan asked.

"Haven't we got this backwards?" A.J. said. "Aren't I supposed to be the one saying yes?"

"Probably, darling, but old habits die hard. And you are pretty accustomed to being in the driver's seat."

A.J. laughed as Dan put his arm around her and led her toward his warm Thunderbird.

"Ask me," she insisted. "Propose to me in the traditional way."

Soberly, lovingly, Dan Barenfanger asked A.J. to marry him.

A.J. realized then what Jill Alexander had known. A.J.'s time as an executive race driver was almost over, and her life as a wife was about to begin. Dan Barenfanger was intent on claiming her for his beloved bride.

"My answer," she said, "is yes!"

A Letter To Our Readers

Dear Reader:

In order that we might better contribute to your reading enjoyment, we would appreciate your taking a few minutes to respond to the following questions and return to:

Karen Carroll, Editor
Heartsong Presents
P.O. Box 719
Uhrichsville, Ohio 44683

1. Did you enjoy reading *Indy Girl*?
   ❑ Very much. I would like to see more books by this author!
   ❑ Moderately
   ❑ I would have enjoyed it more if

   _____

2. Where did you purchase this book?_____

   _____

3. What influenced your decision to purchase this book?
   ❑ Cover   ❑ Back cover copy
   ❑ Title   ❑ Friends
   ❑ Publicity   ❑ Other _____

4. Please rate the following elements from 1 (poor) to 10 (superior).
   - ❑ Heroine   ❑ Plot
   - ❑ Hero   ❑ Inspirational theme
   - ❑ Setting   ❑ Secondary characters

5. What settings would you like to see in Heartsong Presents Books?

   _____

   _____

6. What are some inspirational themes you would like to see treated in future books?

   _____

   _____

7. Would you be interested in reading other Heartsong Presents Books?
   - ❑ Very interested
   - ❑ Moderately interested
   - ❑ Not interested

8. Please indicate your age range:
   - ❑ Under 18   ❑ 25-34   ❑ 46-55
   - ❑ 18-24   ❑ 35-45   ❑ Over 55

Name _____

Occupation _____

Address _____

City _____ State _____ Zip _____

HAVE YOU MISSED ANY OF THESE TITLES?

These additional titles in our Romance Reader series contain two complete romance novels for the price of one. You'll enjoy hours of great inspirational reading. Published at $7.95 each, these titles are available through Heartsong Presents for $3.97 each.

_____ RR2 A MIGHTY FLAME & A CHANGE OF HEART by *Irene Brand*

_____ RR3 LEXI'S NATURE & TORI'S MASQUERADE by *Eilene M. Berger*

_____ RR5 SONG OF JOY & ECHOES OF LOVE by *Elaine Schulte*

_____ RR7 FOR LOVE ALONE & LOVE'S SWEET PROMISE by *Susan Feldhake*

_____ RR9 SUMMER'S WIND BLOWING & SPRING WATERS RUSHING by *Susannah Hayden*

_____ RR10 SECOND SPRING & THE KISS GOODBYE by *Sally Laity*

Great New Inspirational Fiction

from HEARTS♥NG PRESENTS

Biblical Novel Collection #1
by Lee Webber

Two complete inspirational novels in one volume.

_____ **BNC1 CALL ME SARAH**—Can Sarah, like Queen Esther be used by God . . . even as a slave in Herod's place?
CAPERNAUM CENTURION—One Centurion's life is irrevocably changed by his encounter with a certain Nazarene.

CITRUS COUNTY MYSTERY COLLECTION № 1
by Mary Carpenter Reid

Two complete inspirational mystery novels in one volume.

_____ **CCM1 TOPATOPA**—Can Alyson Kendricks make an history village come alive . . . without becoming history herself?
DRESSED FOR DANGER—Roxanne Shelton's fashion designs were the key to her success . . . but did they unlock a closet of secrets?

BOTH COLLECTIONS ARE AVAILABLE FOR $3.97 EACH THROUGH HEARTSONG PRESENTS. ORIGINALLY PUBLISHED AT $7.95 EACH.

LOVE A GREAT LOVE STORY?

Introducing Heartsong Presents —
Your Inspirational Book Club

Heartsong Presents Christian romance reader's service will provide you with four never before published romance titles every month! In fact, your books will be mailed to you at the same time advance copies are sent to book reviewers. You'll preview each of these new and unabridged books before they are released to the general public.

These books are filled with the kind of stories you have been longing for—stories of courtship, chivalry, honor, and virtue. Strong characters and riveting plot lines will make you want to read on and on. Romance is not dead, and each of these romantic tales will remind you that Christian faith is still the vital ingredient in an intimate relationship filled with true love and honest devotion.

Sign up today to receive your first set. Send no money now. We'll bill you only $9.97 post-paid with your shipment. Then every month you'll automatically receive the latest four "hot off the press" titles for the same low post-paid price of $9.97. That's a savings of 50% off the $4.95 cover price. When you consider the exaggerated shipping charges of other book clubs, your savings are even greater!

THERE IS NO RISK—you may cancel at any time without obligation. And if you aren't completely satisfied with any selection, return it for an immediate refund.

TO JOIN, just complete the coupon below, mail it today, and get ready for hours of wholesome entertainment.

Now you can curl up, relax, and enjoy some great reading full of the warmhearted spirit of romance.